MURDER ON HER MIND

MURDER ON HER MIND

VECHEL HOWARD

CUTTING EDGE

ISBN-13: 978-1-962896-95-5

Published by
Cutting Edge Books
PO Box 8212
Calabasas, CA 91372
www.cuttingedgebooks.com

For JOHNNY ROSCOE

CHAPTER ONE

I T WAS SOME high-ranking saint's day, or maybe national car-
penters' or mechanics' or bricklayers' day. Anyhow, it was one
of those Mexican mornings when the dawn was shattered by a
frantic tolling of church bells and fusillades of cannon crackers
and gunfire.

He had left a call for seven when he checked into the leading
hotel of that beautiful town at two that morning, but the celebra-
tion woke him abruptly at six. He lay in bed trying to sleep, until
his phone rang at seven. Then, despite the noise, he did go back to
sleep. It was after nine when he got up, shaved and took a tepid,
inadequate shower in the violet-hued tile bath; then he dressed,
put on a clean shirt and the gray slacks, wrinkled from the long
ride down on the plane. Before he put on his jacket he strapped
on the Magnum. Normally they didn't search your person going
through customs up in Mexico City and he had taken a little
chance and brought his gun along.

The morning was bright, with everything clean and
fresh from the rain the night before and after he had bought
an *Excelsior* at the newsstand he went out on the glassed-in terrace of the hotel and sat down at a table there. He ordered steak
and fried eggs and, while he waited, read the account of O'Dell's
murder in the paper.

The murder of Kimball O'Dell was the reason he was there.

He was eating his steak when a mud-spattered taxi came
along past the pink palace at the end of the plaza, swung around

the corner and stopped in front of the hotel. He saw the blonde girl who got out and she looked so much like his Laura that for a moment his heart stopped. He watched her come onto the terrace and she even walked the way Laura had. She was wearing a wool suit and carrying a raincoat and when she saw him looking at her she returned his gaze for an instant in a direct but distracted way, just long enough to make sure he wasn't anyone she knew; then she went on into the hotel.

A few minutes later he went out and got in the cab the girl had arrived in, which was standing at the curb waiting for a fare. He had the envelope on which old Mrs. O'Dell in San Francisco had written the name and address of her dead son's friend and neighbor. The gentleman's name was Alonzo Mendoza and Johnny told the cab driver the address.

The part of town the taxi went to was full of ups and downs. After a short ride they stopped on a narrow, gently climbing street before a mauve façade and a pair of towering double doors. The church bells were still tolling fitfully and not everyone had run out of firecrackers and ammunition yet. Just after Johnny had lifted the great bronze knocker on one of the doors and let it fall, a bullet whispered past his head, the lead spattering and whining on the stone arch that framed the doors.

He whirled and looked up the street, saw slumlike warrens of old brick rising beneath the blue, burning sky; then one of the great double doors opened and without delay he stepped through to find himself in a paved court where a fountain played and there were large tropical birds tethered in small, surrealistic-looking trees.

The door had been opened by a porter wearing sandals, white pajama-like pants and a white coat. "Señor Church?" he asked, having difficulty with the name.

Johnny was surprised. "Yes," he said. He followed the man across the court to a living room, an airy, open, Moorish dream of a room that looked out upon a small pear-shaped swimming pool and there a butler met him, an elderly Mexican in a colored vest who uttered his name, took his card and motioned him to follow. Johnny followed out onto a terrace, and after the drab, fog-shrouded demitints of San Francisco he felt drunk with the color—of sky, manicured grass and bougainvillea.

They approached some lime-tinted, louvered doors that opened upon the terrace and the man said to Johnny, "*Un momento, por favor,*" and he stepped through the doors which were ajar. True to his word, in a moment he reappeared and waved Johnny into the room.

Johnny Church would never forget the scene that met his eyes as he stepped through those doors. Though the decor was certainly not the first thing to rivet his attention, the classic beauty of that bedchamber he entered was certainly important, for in any other setting the tableau that he saw, though interesting, would have been absurd. And, with the late Kim O'Dell's friend, Alonzo Mendoza, he was to learn, nothing was ever absurd; fantastic, perhaps, but then so was Mendoza.

The floor of the room was composed of huge blocks of pinkish stone and on it were two magnificent Oriental rugs. On one side of the room a shaft of light from a high lattice window streamed in to fall upon a large Rivera painting, a nude dating from the painter's impressionist days. Beyond the painting were shelves of fine, leather-bound gold-tooled books. On the other side of the room were a fireplace and an Empire desk over which hung a gallery of photographs. In the foreground there were great fluffy white chairs and a couch, marble-topped tables, silver objects, inlaid boxes, the whole effect being one of overwhelming elegance. Yet all this was nothing, for the immediate and compelling focus of attention, centered on the great canopied bed which, like a monument or a shrine, was mounted on a dais in the very center of the room.

Reclining on that monstrous bed, propped up by a small snowdrift of pillows, lay a magnificent-looking white-haired man in a burgundy-colored silk dressing gown. He was eating fruit from a silver tray which was being held for him by a young Mexican girl who had one of the loveliest bodies Johnny Church had ever seen. Since the girl had nothing on there was ample opportunity to make such a judgment. She was on her knees beside the bed, her golden buttocks resting on her heels, her torso erect, high breasts pointing obliquely, head bent, her arms lifted up and outward to hold the tray.

"Good morning!" the man on the bed called effervescently to Johnny, and his English was very English. "I am Alonzo Mendoza, Mr. Church." He popped a grape into his mouth and glanced at Johnny's card, then he read aloud from the card. "Gerard Secret Service. Nation-wide Detective Work. Offices in Principal Cities." He regarded Johnny once more. "You're *manager* of the San Francisco office, I see. Nothing but the best for O'Dell."

"No," said Johnny. "It wasn't entirely that. I'm the only one in my office who speaks Spanish." He made an effort to keep his gaze on Mr. Mendoza, but that was impossible. He looked at the girl again. "Doesn't she get tired?"

Mendoza seemed surprised by the question. "It's her *work*," he replied rather sharply. He glanced at the girl, then made a languid gesture of dismissal and she got up and vanished with the tray.

For her I'd find better work, Johnny thought, but he didn't mention it. He sat down on the white couch, feeling giddy from so much sudden strangeness, trying to get his mind operating again, to start earning his pay.

"I read the account in this morning's *Excelsior*," he said. "Robbery seems to be out. About all the police seem to have is that he was found early yesterday morning in his bedroom shot through the head. And he didn't do it himself. Is that right?"

"If the police know any more than that they haven't told me," said Mr. Mendoza. "The police—and not oddly—are very sluggish about finding people who dupe, rob or even kill Americans. If a Mexican is guilty it's bad publicity. *Tourismo* doesn't like it. And if one American does something to another, like killing him, that's more or less their own affair. Investigations in such cases are, to say the least, apathetic. And, anyhow, Mr. Church—" He broke off, gazing at Johnny. "By the way," he asked, "how old are you?"

"Thirty-one," Johnny told him.

"Well, that seems very young to me," Mr. Mendoza said. "It would seem to me that one that age couldn't really know much of life; but, of course, I could be wrong."

"You could be," Johnny told him. Where was this double talk getting them?

"In any event," Mr. Mendoza continued, "I was about to say that down here life is very cheap. It's not the way it is up there in the States, where you spend all sorts of time, money and medicine trying to keep a lot of senile, ridiculous people alive. And always flying serums somewhere to save some stricken one. And *breeding!* Making *more* of the same all the time! Building new rows of hideous houses to accommodate the overflow. Oh, I tell you, Mr. Church, sometimes when I look at those vapid, simpering faces in your advertisements it makes me ill."

"That's your privilege, sir," Johnny told him. Then he said, "Who do you think killed O'Dell?"

"Now, now!" Mr. Mendoza warned, wagging a forefinger. "That's your job. I can tell you I was delighted when Mrs. O'Dell phoned me back after I had told her the sad tidings and said she was sending a detective down. I've been most eagerly awaiting your arrival, Mr. Church."

Johnny gazed thoughtfully at him. He was beginning to get rather accustomed to him, if that were really possible. For a moment he studied Mr. Mendoza's face and, meanwhile, the old gentleman studied him. It was the face of a Spanish grandee he saw there on the bed, Johnny decided. Then suddenly the girl with the tray made sense.

"Down here," Mr. Mendoza declared, "only the most hardy ones survive. It's got to be that way to keep the birthrate down. If you coddle the unfit you're bound to end up with a nation of happy morons. Life is *too* abundant! We know that here. Here you can have somebody you don't like killed for a couple of hundred pesos—less than twenty dollars to you. Despite the religious fol-do-rol, death here, like life, just does not have the fateful, magnified importance, that precious sanctity, regardless of quality, that you people give it."

Birthrate! Johnny thought. This has gone far enough. At the speed I'm making now I'll be all week just getting out of this room. "Now," he said briskly, taking out a notebook, "Mrs. O'Dell seemed sure that you would cooperate with me, sir. I had to catch a plane, so there wasn't much time to talk to her."

"Talk to me!" said Mr. Mendoza. "There's absolutely nothing that I can't tell you. I know everybody. I know all *about* everybody—and I am particularly well informed in respect to my late neighbor and friend, the much loved Kim O'Dell. Just ask me your questions, Mr. Church. I not only know everything that goes on, but I am intensely interested in all of it. Life to me is a fascinating, constantly changing carpet of many colors on which an intricate and beautiful design is constantly changing. And each little part of that design affects all the other parts!"

"Yes, sir," said Johnny. "Let's try to get some facts straight now."

"Good!" agreed Mr. Mendoza. "Let's begin then. I should tell you that I also had a telephone call yesterday from Mr. Jervis Ross in San Francisco. Mr. Ross and Mrs. Maybrick will be down some time today."

Johnny glanced at the notebook where he had jotted down the things old lady O'Dell had told him. "That would be Mr. O'Dell's lawyer," he said.

"Know him well," Mr. Mendoza remarked. "He's been down often. He and Kim were at Princeton together."

"And Mrs. Maybrick is O'Dell's ex-wife—his last one," said Johnny. "I understand she has custody of their boy. She left O'Dell to marry a man named Maybrick and recently she got a divorce from him. In fact, she came down here to get her divorce just last month."

"All correct," agreed Mr. Mendoza. He watched Johnny replace the notebook in his pocket. "How much do you weigh?" he asked him.

"A hundred and eighty," Johnny said. "Why?"

"I was just thinking that you make quite a large target," Mr. Mendoza mused. "Another thing—why do you have your hair cut so short?"

"Then I don't have to comb it."

"How did you happen to become a detective, Mr. Church? I'm very curious. Did you take a course in it, or something? Do you have a degree—Doctor of Detection—a D.D., perhaps?"

Johnny said, making no effort now to conceal his exasperation, "I would prefer not to go into that at this time. You say you want to co-operate with me—"

"Oh, I do!" Mr. Mendoza declared. "But the better I know you, my dear fellow, the better I *can* co-operate. Therefore, these little personal questions."

"All right," Johnny said after a moment. "Let's start again. I asked you who you thought might have killed O'Dell. I got no co-operation from you on that question. Now I'm going to rephrase the question. Do you know anyone who had a motive, any good reason to kill O'Dell?"

"And again I object!" exclaimed Mr. Mendoza. "If you are going to play this game we must have some rules. Facts, even hearsay, gossip and background material, all this I will furnish you, but I reserve the right to keep my suppositions and suspicions to myself, just as I'm sure that you will expect to enjoy the privacy of your own—when you acquire any."

Johnny gazed at him a long moment, at the great white-maned head, noting how immaculately cut and combed the thick hair was, the small but remarkably expressive brown eyes, the thin-lipped line of the mouth, at once quizzical and autocratic, the old man's whole effect of being fantastic and regal. He would, Johnny guessed, be sixty-five or so, and he was remarkably vital looking and well preserved.

"Well, all right," Johnny said reluctantly, "I don't want to ask you to put the finger on anybody. Just tell me about O'Dell's life here, who his friends were, anything you can tell me that you think might have some connection with his death. After that I'd like to look at that bedroom of his, where they found him. Then I'll talk to the police." He leaned back and lit a cigarette and as he did he saw a flicker of movement, someone passing soundlessly in the corridor beyond the archway through which the girl had vanished.

And for a moment then he couldn't help thinking of the girl, seeing that splendid golden body again, and he wondered if that was all she did—serve the fruit that way.

CHAPTER TWO

IT WAS TRUE that he had never met anyone like Mendoza, but when Mendoza began talking about Kim O'Dell he felt that he was on familiar ground again; for he did know the rich, especially the idle rich. They were the ones who hired private detectives.

O'Dell, said Mendoza, had arrived in Mexico twenty years before with the second of the four beautiful women he had wed and divorced during his lifetime. Kim O'Dell had then been a man in his early thirties. He had fallen in love with Mexico, and Alonzo Mendoza had sold him his own magnificent home, after rebuilding this place next door for himself. Both buildings had once been part of an old convent and still shared a common back entrance on a side street.

"So discreet and convenient for the ladies," Mendoza said. "That back entrance." He waved a hand, casting an arch glance at the gallery of photographs above the Empire desk.

The photographs, as Johnny had already noticed, were all of women, young, good-looking women. "Did you share the ladies also?" Johnny inquired mildly.

"*Share?*" Mendoza sounded as if he were turning the word over and peering critically beneath it. "No," he said, rejecting it. "You might say that ladies were our mutual sport, at least during the periods when Kim O'Dell had no wife in residence. But we each chose our own."

"Did O'Dell have any particular lady friend?"

"As of the date of death, he had three of them," the old man answered. "Kim entertained constantly, had people in for lunch every day, dinner every evening, if he didn't go out himself. One or the other of the ladies would act as his hostess when he entertained. He rotated them. Until night before last, Saturday night, he had never brought all three together, or even two."

Johnny asked, "What was his reason for bringing the ladies together Saturday night?"

"It was his birthday," said Mendoza. "And today he had planned to fly up to San Francisco on business, expected to be gone quite some time. So the gathering was also in the way of a farewell. It was very cozy, just the three ladies, Kim and myself."

"Mrs. O'Dell didn't mention that he planned to come up there," Johnny remarked.

"He was going to surprise her," said Mendoza. He gazed reflectively at one foot for a moment, then looked back at Johnny.

The piece about the murder in *Excelsior* had reported that O'Dell's servants left shortly after serving dinner to attend an all-night fiesta in the nearby village of Tepoztlan. O'Dell's valet had returned shortly after dawn Sunday morning and found the body. Now Johnny asked the reclining Mendoza, who continued to gaze at him with a fixed and lively regard: "What time did the party break up?"

"At midnight," said Mendoza. "With the servants away it was not convenient to send the ladies home in one of the cars, so we phoned for three *libres* and dispatched them. Afterward I chatted with Kim a few moments and said good-night."

"Returned here?"

"To this bed," declared Mendoza.

"What were O'Dell's relations with the three ladies?" Johnny asked.

Alonza Mendoza loosed a gleeful chuckle: "Do you mean did he roll in the hay with them?"

"Exactly," Johnny told him.

"Then why not say so!" Mendoza exclaimed. "To be sure he did! What else are the ladies for? He was a regular bull in the boudoir. Kim O'Dell was a vigorous, ardent, life-long devotee of the pleasures comely females come equipped to provide. All *cohones*, you know. That was O'Dell. You do have the *lengua*, don't you? Such a manly chap. I mean to say I don't think he ever went to bed alone. Heavens—I'll bet he's lonely now!"

"I should suppose then maybe one of the ladies returned Saturday night," said Johnny.

"Sound reasoning, dear boy," Mendoza remarked, smiling.

"You wouldn't know which lady, would you?"

"No," said Mendoza slowly.

"Could you maybe guess?"

From his reclining figure now one silk-sheathed arm lifted. A forefinger was waggled, and on that hand there was a ruby that looked as big as the buttons on Johnny's jacket. "Now, now," Mendoza cautioned him. "Remember the rules." The hand fell to rest on a push bell beside the bed, chimes tinkled in the corridor beyond the archway and the elderly Mexican in the brightly colored vest entered.

Mendoza rose from the bed and the servant removed his gown, revealing his lean figure to be clad in a yellow shirt with white ruffles and violet-colored linen trousers. These, having noticed them beneath the dressing gown, Johnny had supposed were pajamas.

While Mendoza stood before a mirror adjusting the white stock at his throat his man entered a dressing room and came out with a white linen jacket. Mendoza slipped into the jacket and picked up a gold-headed cane. He surveyed himself another moment in the mirror, then turned with a flourish.

"*Now*—" he announced. "On to O'Dell's!"

There was a door at one end of the terrace that Mendoza's bedroom and living room opened on. Passing through that door they came into another court, quite large, with firewood stacked neatly at one end, also with great double doors in the wall. In one of the double doors a smaller door had been cut. Mendoza went over and opened the smaller door and Johnny saw that it opened on a narrow side street which ran into the street that Mendoza's house fronted upon.

"You see," said Mendoza, pointing at still another door in the wall of the court behind Johnny, "that leads into O'Dell's. The same key fits both that door and this one leading to the street. Most convenient, you see. The ladies could telephone for a taxi to be waiting here at my corner; then, before dawn caught them, and without walking all the way down to O'Dell's front gate, they could slip out here."

"Could they also slip in?" Johnny asked him. "Did the ladies have keys?"

"They did," said Mendoza. "It was customary at the end of an affair to turn in one's key. If, for some reason, a lady failed to, Kim changed the locks. He told me Saturday he had instructed the locksmith to come today and change them. Since he was only going away for a time, and not really terminating his romances with the ladies, he hadn't wanted to ask them to turn in their keys."

Mendoza pulled shut the street door and crossed the court. He unlocked the door in the wall separating his property from O'Dell's, then he stepped aside for Johnny to precede him. Johnny passed through the door and stopped, and for a moment the three ladies with their keys and the dead O'Dell vanished entirely from his mind.

There, in the heart of that small Mexican city, the scene he gazed upon seemed fabulous beyond belief, a paradise in miniature, sufficient unto itself, and existing in neither time nor place. After stepping through the door he found himself standing upon an eminence of ancient flagging, each dark red stone at least two feet square, mellowed by sun and worn by generations of passing feet. On his right a series of steps, terraces and walks descended gently to a great court with doors opening on the street below. The house was an L, tilted, elongated, shielded from the little side street, where the common entrance was, by a great wall, and in the central area there were banana, avocado and lime trees, brilliantly blossoming shrubs, flower gardens and a blue, limpid pool. He could see the pillars of a great open living room and there were birds singing in the trees and two gardeners, using shards of broken bottles as cutting tools, were trimming the grass around the boles of the trees. Another man, a porter in a white coat, had just opened the umbrella that shaded a big glass-topped table beside the pool. Johnny watched him putting down brightly colored pads on the old stones beside the pool, then the men went over to a bar table that stood against a wall, took a silver ice bucket from it and started down the stairs.

"The king is dead," said Mendoza. "Long live the king. He is gone, yet they know nothing but to go on as they have always done." He paused, gazing out and down, as Johnny was. "*Muy bella*, is it not?" There was real love in his voice.

"*Bellísima!*" said Johnny.

"This was only one of several houses I once had," said Mendoza. "My father, and the fathers before my father, from the time of Cortez, were great *haciendados*, with lands to the east, where we raised cattle, and to the south where we had cane and sugar mills. When I was young, Señor Church, we had other homes—in Ciudad Mexico, Paris, London, Venice. And when I travelled in those days I travelled on my private train, my yacht. This house I built from the old *convento*, utilizing the old stone, the Colonial beams. This house was my gem."

Johnny took a deep breath. Wealth could be nice, he thought. He turned to Mendoza. "Where is O'Dell's bedroom?"

Mendoza pointed with his cane. The bedroom, it seemed, was there in that upper wing, at the base of the L-shaped establishment just above the pool. "No one has touched anything since the police left," Mendoza assured him. "Mrs. O'Dell told me that was your wish." Having said this, he tucked his cane beneath one arm, clapped his hands loudly and bellowed for his valet.

The man instantly appeared on a terrace below. He saw them, started racing up toward them through shafts of tree-filtered sunlight. Mendoza whipped out his keys then. He turned and unlocked a carved door set deep in the fortress-like plastered wall.

O'Dell's bedroom was paneled in some blond native wood, tiled with the highly waxed ancient convent stones, and rugless. There was a fireplace with a carved stone mantel flanked by couches with covers of tailored corduroy. There was a great bed and a large desk with a typewriter on it, a built-in radio-phonograph. On the fireplace wall there were shelves of books. And there were paintings, good ones by the Mexican moderns, and in niches here and there were ancient Aztec and Toltec statuettes, stone vases and other *objets d'art*. It was a very large room and its atmosphere hinted at a hidden Gothic spirit in the late O'Dell.

There was a balcony at the rear of the room where the sun streamed in through opened glass doors and framed the burning southern distance into which the mauve-colored mountains of Guerrero rose. Suddenly there was a shrill, feline sound and a

Siamese cat, which had been crouched in the flowering vine on the parapet, leaped down and came charging tiger-like into the room.

Mendoza gave a start, then said, "Ah—Kim's cat, Oscar Wilde. He's queer and supposedly quite gifted."

The cat came to a stop before Johnny, arched his back, gave a yowl and stared up at him with penetrating amethyst eyes. "Hello, Oscar," Johnny said. He gazed at the unmade bed.

A man in a striped vest came in and bowed. "This is Arturo," Mendoza told Johnny. "Kim's man." And to the man he said in Spanish, "This is Mr. Church. He is a detective from the States."

Johnny had moved to the bed and was looking at the bed linen. There were monograms on the pillow cases, the initials K.O.'D., and there was a trace of lipstick on one. *Which lady?* he wondered. He gazed at the lipstick until he felt he knew the shade. Then, against the dead white sheet, he saw a hair, black, short and curly.

"What did the police do?" he asked.

"Smoked Kim's cigars, asked some questions and dug a bullet out of the wall." Mendoza pointed with his cane and Johnny saw where the paneling had been gouged and splintered on the far side of the bed.

He didn't have to ask where the body had been; the blood had pooled on the stone floor near where he stood. Someone had entered that room with a gun, *Excelsior* had surmised—brilliantly enough—in its story that morning. And, though O'Dell kept a revolver in the drawer of the night table beside his bed there had apparently been no time to get it. O'Dell had apparently snatched up a letter opener from the table and lunged at the intruder. The letter opener had been clutched in his hand when they found him. Johnny opened the drawer of the night table and saw the revolver, picked it up. It was a .38, fully loaded. Despite the urgency, he thought, O'Dell might better have gone for the gun.

Mendoza had seated himself now on one of the couches, his hands were clasped on the head of his cane and he was leaning forward, watching Johnny intently.

Johnny crossed and sat on the couch opposite him and the cat came and rubbed against his leg. "Did you tell the police about the ladies?"

"I only told them who was present Saturday night," Mendoza said. "I have made sure that there will be no publicity. Unless, of course—" He shrugged and waved a hand.

Johnny looked at Arturo. "Is the bed linen changed each day?" he asked in Spanish.

"Yes, sir. Each day," Arturo said. He was slight and young, but he had the quiet assurance of a man who knew his job and did it well.

Once more according to *Excelsior*, when Arturo returned from Tepoztlan early Sunday morning, he had noticed that the door of O'Dell's bedroom was open. It was just past six o'clock and, since it was very unusual for O'Dell's bedroom door to be open at that hour, Arturo had investigated and found the body. Medical opinion was that O'Dell had been shot between two and three o'clock Sunday morning. The bullet had entered the forehead just above the right eye and come out the back of the head.

Johnny had memorized what facts there were in the newspaper article. Now he said to Arturo, "Did your *patrón* usually lock his bedroom door?"

"No, señor," Arturo said.

Johnny took out his notebook and pencil. He looked at Mendoza. "Will you give me the names of those ladies?" he asked him. "I'd like to talk to them."

"Gladly," said Mendoza. "Which do you prefer, Mr. Church—blondes, brunettes, or redheads?"

"I don't pick them by the color of their hair," Johnny said. "If there is a brunette, though, I'll start with her."

"Why?" Mendoza asked quickly.

Johnny leaned back. Oscar Wilde was half under the skirt of the Corduroy cover on Mendoza's couch. He was playing with something. "O'Dell was a blond," he said.

"How do you know?" Mendoza asked. "Did I tell you that? Was there a picture in the paper?"

"I saw a photograph of him at his mother's house in San Francisco," Johnny told him. "When he was a young man."

"Gentlemen prefer *blondes*," Mendoza said. "I have observed many gentlemen, and it's true. I know *I* do."

"It's my impression that blond men often prefer brunettes," Johnny said. He held his pencil ready to write. "What's her name?"

"Rowena King," Mendoza told him. "And now, for each lady, I shall supply a brief dossier. As much as I know, that is. Since I prefer the fillies from my own stable, I can't, I fear, tell you how good any one of the three is in the hay. But Miss King, I should think, shows most promise of excellence there. She's well endowed with the equipment, and she has the necessary fire. She comes from Southern California, has that nebulous background common to so many of your people there. Who asks from whence they came, who their fathers were? They are simply *there*, isn't it so? An entirely new and anonymous race of beings, sprung from the dragon teeth of your vaunted progress!"

Well, here we go again, Johnny thought. "All right," he said. "Thank you. Where will I find the lady?"

"Arturo—" Mendoza said, and his voice was like the casual flicking of a whip.

"The Señora King?" said Arturo quickly, and he was able to furnish, not only the address, but her telephone number.

"She married and divorced some money, I believe," Mendoza went on. "Arrived here several months ago with her mother and a child. Now she's about to marry a lot more money. He's in Paris on business and when he comes back they are to be married here. Kim was to have been best man."

"Next?" Johnny said.

"Eleanor Staples," Mendoza told him. He watched him write the name. "A redhead.

"Natural?"

"I never inquired," Mendoza said. "*She* does have some background, comes from a good Southern family. Married and divorced—twice, I believe. She came down with some other people last summer, one a man who knew Kim. The other people left but she stayed on. I think she really thought Kim would marry her. When Irene Maybrick was down last month she said Eleanor told her that she and Kim were going to get married."

"Do you think they were?"

"It's possible," Mendoza admitted. "Kim had never tried marrying a redhead, and he was a man who would always try anything once."

Johnny glanced inquiringly over at Arturo, who promptly gave him the red-haired lady's address and phone number. "Next?" said Johnny.

"Helen Wellington—very lovely, very young, a luscious blonde." Alonzo Mendoza kissed his fingertips and tossed the kiss into the air. "I wish I had seen that blonde first," he declared. "She was the most recent acquisition to Kim's stable, been here only three weeks. Now let's see about her—she's divorced, of course, but I really don't know much else. She comes from one of those monstrous, terribly ugly, Midwestern cities of yours."

Once more Arturo supplied an address and telephone number, a hotel this time. And, as Johnny wrote, he was aware again of the sounds that Oscar Wilde was making beneath the other couch. It sounded as if Oscar were playing with a marble. Then, just as he closed his notebook, and while Alonzo Mendoza dabbed at his nose and mouth with a scented yellow silk handkerchief, the Siamese cat burst forth from the corduroy couch skirt and came racing across the polished stone floor toward Johnny like a hockey player nursing a puck toward the goal.

The puck, in this case, was a camera flashbulb. Oscar propelled it to Johnny's feet, then he sat and gazed up with those baleful, amethyst eyes, as if to say, "Well, now—what do you make of this!"

Johnny leaned over and picked up the flashbulb. It was an unused one, a Number 5.

Perhaps if he hadn't been in the business, if so much of the agency work had not involved obtaining photographic evidence and so many of the cases had not involved blackmail, the flashbulb would have meant nothing. And later on he was to think it would have been better if it *had* meant nothing. As it was, even though he could not fit the flashbulb—used or unused—into any given situation connected with the death of O'Dell, it still suggested a situation.

"Was O'Dell a camera bug?" he asked Mendoza sharply.

Mendoza shook his head. It was clear that he was interested and puzzled by the bulb; and so, Johnny saw, was Arturo. "No, he wasn't a camera bug," Mendoza said. "He had cameras. He used, some time ago, to take photographs on trips, but—" He snapped over his shoulder at Arturo, "What about this?"

"I never saw this bulb," Arturo said. "I know nothing of it."

"Are you sure the police didn't take a picture of the body?" Johnny asked Mendoza.

"Positive," said Mendoza.

Johnny got down on his knees. He lifted the skirt of the couch he had been sitting on and looked under it, then he looked under the couch where Oscar Wilde had found the flashbulb, and there was not even any dust beneath the couches.

"The bulb was not beneath that couch Saturday morning, señor," Arturo told him. "I personally supervised the cleaning of this room. The couches were moved and the women mopped the floors."

"Will you show me your master's cameras?" Johnny asked.

"Yes, señor." Arturo crossed the room and opened a door. The door led into a small semi-circular area where sporting guns were locked behind glass and steel mesh in a cabinet. In another cabinet various types of Mexican knives were displayed. Arturo opened a felt-lined drawer. He took out several expensive German cameras and put them on a table. He brought out the light meters, the lenses, everything in the drawer, and, among the boxes there was one containing a flash attachment. The Number 5 bulb, however, did not fit it.

"You place importance on that flashbulb, don't you? Mendoza asked as Johnny came back.

Johnny tossed up the bulb and caught it, then he dropped it into his jacket pocket. "I only want it explained how it got here," he said. "The explanation may not be important."

Mendoza rose. "Well now—I must be off to the mortuary," he declared briskly. "I must see what they've done with him." He levelled his cane at Arturo. "What is the time?"

Arturo studied his big Mexican wrist watch and announced that it was twenty-five minutes past ten o'clock and just as he finished saying so, there was the distant silvery tinkling of a bell somewhere below them.

"Come with me and see O'Dell," Mendoza told Johnny.

"I want to go and talk to the police right now", Johnny said.

They were walking from the room as they spoke and when they came out upon the burning stones of the terrace above the pool they could hear the dull iron clanging of a bolt below them; then one of the great doors of the lower court was swung inward by a porter and a man and a woman entered. The Siamese cat sprang to a walltop below the pool and yowled and Alonzo Mendoza plucked his yellow handkerchief from the breast pocket of his jacket and began to wave it.

"It's Jervis and Irene," Mendoza said. He tied the handkerchief to the end of his cane and began to wave it like a flag.

That would be O'Dell's lawyer and his ex-wife just arrived from San Francisco down there in the court, Johnny thought. He decided then to wait. And, as a matter of fact, he realized that he *did* want to see O'Dell. It would make things less ghostly and strange for him, he felt, if he could take a look at the departed satyr's face.

CHAPTER THREE

T HE LADY HAD ON her San Francisco clothes, a mink stole and a hand-knit suit. Her companion was one of those debonair, aging boy-men, the custom cashmere kind, yet with wisps of alma mater's ivy still clinging after all these years in the cut of his clothes, his tie. They looked as if they had just stepped out of the Hotel St. Francis or maybe the Waldorf into that exotic courtyard, Johnny thought. And, this time, the boys up there in the Madison Avenue advertising agencies had got their copy mixed, he decided; the people were all right—the same couple you saw last month in that *Town and Country* ad—but the background was all wrong. Against the burning beauty of that scene their false and careful perfection was grotesque.

He watched them grow from miniatures to life-size people as they ascended the effortless gradient of steps, walks and terraces. They came along by the pool, their passing strangeness reflected by limpid water, and now two pretty maids in immaculate white had come from the house to join the porter who carried the bags, and Oscar Wilde had leaped from his wall, yowling what sounded like insults as he followed the procession up onto that ultimate terrace of the many-splendored house.

Alonzo Mendoza gave Irene Maybrick a Mexican-style embrace and kissed her cheek. He shook Jervis Ross's hand.

For Irene Maybrick, Johnny saw, that terrace was a stage and her part called for a noble show of female fortitude. From her demeanor you could see that she wished to make clear to everyone that though her heart was breaking with grief and shock she was bearing up just wonderfully under it all. Her performance was so hammy that Johnny couldn't help grinning and when he did her cold green eyes shot little cold green daggers at him. Then she said to Mendoza, with just the faintest burble of a sob in her voice, "Where is he?"

"Who?" Mendoza inquired.

"Kim."

"Oh—" said Mendoza. "The mortician has him."

Now Johnny saw that lawyer Ross was looking him over. Ross looked at his shoes, at his wrinkled slacks, his jacket, his necktie. Ross looked at his face, and at his hair, but he never established eye contact. He looked at Johnny as if he were just some large, slightly puzzling object that one must step around in order to get into O'Dell's bedroom.

O'Dell's bedroom was where they were going. While the servants, supervised by Arturo, took their luggage into other bedrooms, the two flowed around Johnny and, followed by Mendoza and the cat, passed through the door behind him. And now the bell in the great lower court tinkled once more and Johnny saw the porter go racing down to admit two straw-hatted figures, an elderly Mexican and a little boy carrying a satchel; then he heard Alonzo Mendoza call his name and he turned and re-entered the bedroom.

Mendoza had seated himself once more on the near couch. Irene Maybrick had dropped her purse and stole on the coffee table between the couches and now she was pacing, hands clasped, high heels clicking a slow cadence on the old stones. Jervis Ross had wandered over to the big desk and was standing gazing down at the things on the desk. Mendoza was leaning forward, his hands on his cane, watching them.

"This is Mr. Church, the detective Kim's mother sent down," Mendoza said.

Mrs. Maybrick had gone to the opened balcony doors. Now she turned, swept the room with a tragic, green glance and said, "It seems incredible he's not here somewhere. This room *is* Kim."

"Only the furnishings, my dear," Mendoza corrected her. "Don't forget I created this room." He looked at Johnny. "In the old convent days this was where they made their cheese," he said.

Irene looked at Johnny then, too, and so did Ross. "I don't suppose you've had time to come to a conclusion of any sort," Ross said to him.

"No," Johnny said.

"How about the police?" Ross asked Mendoza. "Do they have anything more than what was in the newspapers?"

"I don't know," Mendoza told him. "Mr. Church is going to talk to the police."

Jervis Ross sat down in the leather-upholstered chair behind the desk. "Well," he declared, "there's going to be a lot to do."

Ross was bald, and he was one of those men who looked as if he always had been bald. His head was nicely shaped and the gray wings of hair that remained above his ears had waves in them and were brushed straight back. He was tan, obviously fit, quite competent looking too. And his blue gaze when it hit you directly, Johnny found, had a certain unexpected force. As Johnny watched him he put on a pair of glasses and opened the center drawer of the desk. "Mrs. O'Dell said she told you to make arrangements for shipping the remains up there," he said to Mendoza.

"I have done so," Mendoza said. "I am going to pop over for a look at him and, if I approve of what has been done, off he flies to his mother. Would you two like to come along and see him?"

"No," Irene said quickly. "I don't want to see him."

Mendoza then glanced at Ross. "How about you, Jervis?"

"I would prefer to skip it too," Jervis Ross said. "I suppose I ought to fly back up there for the funeral. But I don't know. Right now I want to start going through Kim's papers. He was in some things down here I wasn't handling for him. I'll have to see what's involved." He bent his head, staring thoughtfully into the drawer he had opened.

Irene Maybrick, Johnny saw, was sending Mendoza a message. She swiveled her eyes and inclined her head meaningfully toward the balcony, then Johnny watched her turn and walk the length of the room once more to the opened balcony doors.

They were always too thin, he thought—at least for his taste—the Irene Maybricks. And he did not like the way they walked. His Laura had walked like poetry; Irene Maybrick walked as if her pelvis had been frozen.

Mendoza rose, lifted his cane high and winked at him. "*Un momentito, Señor Church*," he said, and he followed Irene.

Jervis Ross pushed some papers around in the drawer, then he picked up a small leather notebook and riffled the pages. He tossed the notebook back and pulled the drawer farther out, leaning forward to peer into the back of it. "You're a detective," he told Johnny. "Where would a man be apt to jot down the combination to his safe?"

"He might not," Johnny told him. "He might just keep it in his head."

"That's what I'm afraid of," Jervis Ross said. He got up and went to a small painting on the wall beyond the desk. The painting was of a girl with a basket on her head and when Ross pulled at it a section of panelling slid aside to reveal the steel face of a large, combination safe set in the wall. Beside the safe was a steel filecase which also had a less complicated combination lock.

Ross tried a drawer of the filecase, he gave a tug at the knob of the safe, then he frowned and looked at Johnny. "This is a pretty kettle of smelt," he declared. He turned and strode back to the desk, began pulling open other drawers.

He could open that filecase, Johnny thought, like he could a can of beans. The safe, though, would be a different proposition. He went to the filecase and spun the knob of the combination a couple of times, then he began at zero, and dialed slowly left, listening to the tumblers.

A few minutes later he had it. He pulled the top drawer open a few inches and when he turned he saw Jervis Ross down on the floor examining the underside of the big center drawer of the desk. He went over and wrote the combination of the filecase on the back of an envelope lying on the desk and when Ross got up off his knees he handed the envelope to him.

"Why—you opened it!" Ross said in a genuinely surprised voice.

"I got lucky," Johnny told him.

"How about the safe?"

"That I wouldn't tackle. I might open it in a couple of days, but I don't have a couple of days."

"Well, I'll have to get in that safe too—somehow," Ross said. He moved over to the file, pulled the top drawer all the way out and started looking through the folders, and it was clear to Johnny that he was looking for something in particular.

"Mr. Church—"

Johnny turned and saw Mendoza step in spryly from the balcony. "Mrs. Maybrick wishes a word with you!" Mendoza told him; then he saw Ross at the open filecase and he forgot Johnny. He moved over and sat on the edge of the desk, watching Ross.

Oscar Wilde was in the vine when Johnny stepped out onto the balcony. Oscar stared at him through flaming blossoms with a terrible intensity, as if to say, "If only you knew what *I* know, Señor Church!"

Irene Maybrick was tall, about five-eight and she had an arrogant lower lip. She wore a little blue cloche that matched her shoes and the buttons on the knit suit. Her thick dark hair gleamed in the sun like wet sealskin and her eyes, narrowed against that hot light, created a tiny fanlike pattern of wrinkles high on her cheeks. Still he could recognize her beauty, though it was not the kind for him.

"Yes, ma'am?" he said. She was holding a cigarette and he lit it for her with his lighter, meeting her gaze.

"It was an inside job," she said. She threw back her head and nodded at him, smoke curling slowly from her pretty nose.

"Ma'am?" he said.

"I *know*," she declared deeply. "Don't forget I lived down here eight years." Her voice descended to a husky whisper. "I just told Alonzo—it's Arturo. I'll bet you on that, Mr. Church."

"Why would Arturo have wanted to kill Mr. O'Dell?"

"Robbery, naturally. I know these servants down here. They'll steal you blind. We always used to lock everything in the safe, and we'd warn our house guests not to leave valuables lying around. Kim said Arturo was stealing from him when I was down here last winter. He was padding the bills and getting kickbacks from all the merchants. I never did trust that man."

"As far as we know there's nothing missing," Johnny said.

"We may never know what's missing!"

"How do you mean?" he asked.

"I think Arturo learned the combination to that safe. Surely he'd watched Kim open it enough. And who can say now what was in there? Kim always kept big sums of cash. He had gold—in case of a panic, or a revolution or something. Diamonds. I *know*. I was his wife eight long years."

Johnny nodded. "I'll check on it," he said. "I'll see what the police say."

"You do it!" she told him emphatically, then she hurled her cigarette over the parapet and returned to the bedroom.

In the bedroom Mendoza was pounding a bell on the desk and calling for Arturo and when Arturo appeared the old man yelled at him, "Where's that locksmith who was supposed to come change the locks on those doors this morning?"

"He is here, señor," Arturo said. "He is working on the locks now."

"Bring him in here!" Mendoza commanded. He banged his cane on the floor. "Tell him to open that safe."

Jervis Ross was leaning against the filecase. He wanted to get into the safe badly.

Arturo reappeared almost at once, and with him were the straw-hatted man and boy that Johnny had watched the porter admit to the court just after Ross and Mrs. Maybrick arrived. They swept off their hats before they entered and the knowledge of what had happened in that room was in their eyes. Their eyes strayed to the blood on the tiles and they crossed themselves, then the locksmith came on in, bowing politely to everybody and saying, "*Con permiso, señores. Con permiso, señora*," and the little boy ghosted along after him, carrying a satchel of tools, also bowing and asking everyone's permission to be there.

The locksmith, after gazing doubtfully at the safe for a moment put one ear against the door of it and started moving the dial. Ross and Irene Maybrick sat on a couch and Mendoza got off the desk. He looked at Johnny and said, "Now, my friend, we'll go to the mortuary.

Ross's eyes were on Mendoza's face. "I brought a copy of Kim's will down with me," he told him.

"Ah—" Mendoza said slowly.

"Everything goes into a trust fund for the boy, you know."

"Yes, so I understood. So Kim told me," Alonzo Mendoza said.

"There are, however, certain bequests," Ross continued. "I thought you'd be interested to know, Alonzo, that Kim remembered you very handsomely in one of them."

"Oh, the dear chap!" Mendoza exclaimed. "I *never* expected that! Never!"

"He left you his cellar," Jervis Ross said, and his eyes brightened as he watched Mendoza's face.

Mendoza, Johnny saw, had paled. "His *cellar!*" he said in a sick-sounding whisper.

"Kim's cellar has such a magnificent collection of still wines, I remember," Ross remarked.

"And *brandies*," Irene said. "Oh, how very nice for you, Alonzo!" She gave a smothered shout of laughter.

Mendoza whipped out his yellow silk handkerchief and dabbed at his mouth and nose, and his face, Johnny observed, had grown still paler.

"Of course if you don't want the cellar you could dispose of it," Ross said. "I might buy it."

"No!" Mendoza cried. "I won't dispose of it. I shall keep the cellar. And, I tell you—when I'm once more in residence in this house that cellar shall serve all of my guests!"

Having delivered himself of this declamation Mendoza turned and motioned Johnny; then he marched angrily from the room.

Johnny, puzzled by the interchange, followed the old gentleman out of the bedroom and across the stones. They passed through the rear gate and on through Mendoza's house into the street where an immaculate maroon Rolls of ancient vintage awaited them. As they emerged a uniformed chauffeur sprang to open a rear door of the car.

Alonzo Mendoza mounted the running board, pointed his cane and said, "*Quo vadis!*"

That too, thought Johnny as he leaned back on the glovelike leather upholstery, was very peculiar. *Quo vadis*—whither goest thou?

"Why did you quote that Latin?" he asked Mendoza as the car purred smoothly along the broken, cobbled street.

"That," said Alonzo Mendoza, "is the name of the local mortuary." He gave a gleeful chuckle. "Great—isn't it?"

Johnny was silent a moment while they waited for some burros to pass in the narrow street, then he said, "I didn't quite understand that about O'Dell's cellar, either."

"Oh, don't think I can't see the humor of it!" Mendoza assured him. "I like a joke as well as the next fellow—even if it is on me."

"What *was* the joke?"

"I don't drink!" Mendoza exclaimed. "That's the joke. The mere mention of spirits is enough to make me want to vomit!"

After a moment Johnny spoke again. He said, "I gather you plan to buy back your house."

"Correct!" said Mendoza. He smiled and began to crack his knuckles loudly.

Earlier that morning there had been laden trucks parked along the plaza and now a carnival was being set up there under the old laurel trees. Workmen were busy erecting a Ferris wheel, a merry-go-round and an airplane whirligig and several of the amusement stands and the stands selling sweets and food had their canvas up and were already in operation. From the target-shooting tent there came a crackling of rifle fire, somewhere a brassy-voiced speaker was blaring fast and frantic Mexican music and a chorus of automobile horns arose from the clotted traffic. Sandled *campesinos* with great baskets of fruits and vegetables on their backs were streaming through and around the plaza up toward the narrow street that led to the great public market on the hill. There were maids and matrons with shopping baskets on their arms. There were men from the mountains driving burros loaded with firewood, soot-streaked *carboneros*, country people on holiday, strolling maidens with dresses of shrill colors, young men with pomaded hair and peg-top pants, Americans, people right out of the ads, all in gay, tropic attire, all armed with cameras, Spanish dictionaries and great wads of lowly pesos.

As the glittering, vintage Rolls debauched grandly from the cobbled side street into the chaos of the plaza scene Alonzo Mendoza sprang to his feet in the tonneau and began directing things, shouting orders to his own driver, waving his cane menacingly and hurling insults and orders at other drivers. Finally, however, seeing that things were hopelessly snarled, he opened the car door and leaped nimbly to the pavement.

"Come on!" he told Johnny. "We'll hoof it!"

Johnny got out and, dodging burros, cars and people, followed Mendoza across the street into the plaza, and he wished as he rushed along that he weren't on a job down here. He would have liked the time to sit on a bench in the sun and watch everything. As it was, he had a hard time just keeping his agile companion in sight.

As they crossed the street on the other side of the plaza Mendoza whirled and yelled, "*Momentito*, Church!"

Johnny leaned back against the building in the corner and watched him darting and dodging toward a confectionary stand. Then, almost at once, there was a nasty *pinging* sound, a slap of lead against the plastered bricks next to his head and he jumped away from that spot, dodged into the shadowed entrance of the corner store.

For a moment he stood there gazing back across the plaza and now he had the feeling that someone had just dropped an ice cube down between his shoulder blades. Across the plaza there was an old building which was being razed and, until Mendoza came bouncing back, he watched the rectangular black holes where the windows of the building had been. That shot, he knew, could not have been fired from street level without hitting someone else before it got to where he stood.

Mendoza had two little sticks on which there were fuzzy purple balls of spun-sugar candy. He shoved a stick at Johnny, who absently accepted it, then they started up the narrow market street.

One shot, he thought, could be an accident, but not two on the same morning. And that had been a rifle. Why hadn't they hit him? They could have fired again and tagged him even as he jumped.

He gave his candy to a little girl he passed but Mendoza was still nibbling at his as they entered the mortuary, a narrow old building with a painted shield over its entrance on which were the words: *Quo Vadis.*

In a big, cool room beyond the little office and reception room O'Dell was on display, and that was one corpse Johnny was never going to forget. The elaborate coffin was resting on a dais in the center of the room and the head of the coffin had been elevated so that as you entered the room you saw O'Dell lying there grinning at you.

The dead man was wearing evening dress, a white mess jacket and a scarlet cummerbund and the hand that rested on his shirt front held a sparkling Martini glass. The departed one's gray-blond hair was slicked back neatly, and the ends of his jaunty little mustache had been waxed. He looked, Johnny thought, with that frozen smile and his eyes closed as if in thought, like a man who had just forgotten the punch line of one of his favorite jokes.

"Doesn't he look marvelous!" Mendoza exclaimed. "Don't you think his dear old mother will be pleased?"

"I couldn't say," Johnny told him. He turned away.

So, he thought, he had met O'Dell. And, however gay the corpse, there was no overlooking that plugged hole in the forehead, there was no escaping the thought that it could happen to him.

CHAPTER FOUR

T HE POLICE STATION was at one end of an open quadrangle formed by neglected Colonial buildings, all painted in the popular Mexican pink. Johnny paid his cabdriver and walked into the quad and a little boy who had hooked a ride on the rear bumper from Quo Vadis also got off.

There were ragged prisoners making languid passes at the dirt of the quad with bamboo rakes while a sandled guard in an old rust-brown police blouse watched over them with a 1917 Springfield. Three crows were perched on a telephone wire leading into the police station and as Johnny passed beneath the wire one of the crows cawed and flapped its wings, and again Johnny got that icy feeling between his shoulder blades.

It had been bad, off-beat bad, he thought, ever since he had seen the girl walk into the hotel that morning, for she had reminded him of Kansas City. Bullets and death—that's what Kansas City would always mean to him.

His mind had been working during the short ride in the *libre*; and, until he could explain and prove to his own satisfaction that the flashbulb in his pocket had no bearing on O'Dell's death, his thinking was inevitably going to start with it. The flashbulb suggested just one thing to him: blackmail. And that, he had reason to know, was one of the nastier words in the language.

It also seemed inevitable that one of O'Dell's three ladies should be involved. And the lady would have an accomplice.

The bulb at once created a structure of supposition based on previous experience. After a certain number of cases you discovered patterns. Cranks sent the anonymous letters, made the mysterious phone calls, but the ones that took the pictures were an ugly lot; they knew their business, and they carried guns. He had seen the pictures they took, he had taken such pictures himself for evidence of infidelity in divorce actions. And after a few years in the picture business you lost your illusions about the ladies, particularly those with money, and time on their hands.

As for the two rifle shots, those near-lethal misses of the morning, it was Alonzo Mendoza, he figured, who was indirectly responsible for them. Though in many respects Mendoza was indelibly different from anyone else, still he was in other respects a type. He was one of those males in whom women would confide because they would recognize that he possessed a deep and feminine understanding of them. Women, their gossip, their little intrigues, their talk, their clothes, their romances, the whole giddy, shimmering bubble that was their essence, would be the breath of life to Mendoza, Johnny knew. Mendoza would have been on the telephone right after he talked to Mrs. O'Dell in San Francisco yesterday morning. He would have spoken at length to each of the ladies, told them Mrs. O'Dell was sending a detective down.

Even Mendoza's servants had been expecting his arrival, he reflected, and surely they knew why he had come there. The ladies knew—anyone who might be interested knew. And whoever it was who didn't want him there had paid somebody a couple of hundred pesos to give him a hint. "*Quo Vadis* awaits you," those two slugs had whispered, "if you stay."

He told the man behind the desk in the police station that he wished to talk to the chief about the O'Dell case and the man pointed to an open door and said, "You will find Chief Guiterrez in there, señor."

Johnny stepped through the door into a large room where another prisoner was mopping the stone floor. An unshaded bulb hung from the high ceiling and the only furnishings were a bench, a few chairs, a bulletin board and an old oak desk.

The chief of police was sitting behind the desk and he looked up from the newspaper he was reading at the sound of Johnny's footsteps. He was a heavy man with a big, round face, and a brush of graying hair. His blouse was unbuttoned and on one lapel Johnny noticed a Rotary Club button.

Johnny advanced to the desk, presented his card and explained why he was there and the chief looked relieved to hear his Spanish. Johnny told him he had talked with Mendoza and looked at O'Dell's bedroom and, though the chief was polite, Johnny could see that just the mention of O'Dell's name gave him pain.

"This is a bad thing," he told Johnny. "Everybody knew Señor O'Dell. He was a rich man and so the newspapers have big stories." He tapped the paper he had been reading. "It says here that his father made a great fortune in the lumber business up there in California many years ago. Señor Mendoza told me it was ships they made the money in."

"Both, I think," Johnny said.

"Anyhow, señor, O'Dell had no need to work," the chief continued. "He was one of the American *holgazáns*—how do you say?—idle ones. Still he was such a pleasant man, always a gentleman. He never caused me trouble, like so many of the *holgazáns*." He gave a shrug, managed a wary grin. "Not till yesterday."

"Be assured that I don't wish to cause you more trouble," Johnny told him. "I only want to find out what I can for Señor

O'Dell's old mother. And you have my promise that anything you say to me will be considered confidential."

"Many thanks," the chief said. "Some things I try to keep a secret. I do it because the newspapers are such a nuisance in police work. One is looking for a certain man, then the newspapers print the name and one never finds that man. I am looking for a man now—the man who fired this bullet."

The chief opened a drawer of his desk. He took out a flattened slug and tossed it on the desk. "It has been determined that it is .32 caliber," he said. "And now here is what Señor O'Dell had for a weapon." He laid a miniature machete beside the bullet.

"Señor O'Dell used the knife as a letter opener," Chief Guiterrez continued. He leaned back in his chair. "Now here is what I think happened," he said after a moment. "When Señor O'Dell's servants went to the fiesta in Tepoztlan Saturday night one of the cooks, an elderly woman, was left to tend the gate. She lay down on the bed in the porter's room beside the gate where she would hear the bell, and though she says she admitted no one during the night I believe she is lying. Señor Church, that woman has a son who has spent much time in prison. He has been working on a plantation down below Taxco, but on Saturday evening he was seen here in this town and over in Tepoztlan. It is my belief he killed Señor O'Dell."

Johnny gazed at him. "Robbery?"

The chief nodded. "I believe he learned from O'Dell's servants that his mother was tending the gate, that Señor O'Dell was alone in the house. I believe he went there to rob O'Dell and, as so often happens, a greater crime grew from the lesser one that was contemplated." He shrugged. "Who knows exactly what happened? Perhaps I will find that out when I find the man."

"He's vanished?"

The chief gazed at him. "He has not returned to Taxco. We are looking for him."

Johnny nodded. He wouldn't buy it, he thought. And he understood now that the chief didn't think he would. The old cook's son would have been told the police were looking for him, and by the time they did give his name to the papers he would be across the Rio Grande. He would be just another wetback picking cotton up in Texas somewhere. People would forget O'Dell. The case would be, to all intents, solved, for the disappearance of the cook's son would indicate his guilt.

"Did you question the ladies who were present Saturday evening?"

The chief stirred. He leaned forward and laid his big hands flat on the desk. "As a matter of routine only," he said.

And there was a warning now in the chiefs eyes. Johnny knew he was being told: "Don't make any more bad publicity here. We need your tourists. We need your dollars. Don't scare them away."

"With your permission I would like to talk to the ladies," he told the chief. "I assure you I will be most prudent in all I do. My investigation will be strictly private, the results revealed only to my client and, if you desire, to you."

The chief shrugged. "By all means—talk to the ladies." He got up, smiling. "Such work is pleasure." He held out a hand. "Take care, Señor Church," he said, and he wasn't smiling any more; he meant it.

CHAPTER FIVE

E WALKED the few short blocks back to the plaza and stopped before the gutted building. The main doors of the building had been removed and a ramp built over the steps. There were broken bricks and timber stacked against the wall and two mortar-spattered wheelbarrows were tilted up against one side of the ramp.

For a moment he stood listening, and over in the plaza that speaker was still blaring feverish music and, mingled with it now was the familiar refrain of a merry-go-round and the target rifles crackled steadily. But there was no sound inside the building. He could hear no hammering, no voices.

Presently he went up the ramp and stepped into the desolate quiet, into a yawning coolness, an acrid atmosphere of brick and lime dust. Another ramp led to the second floor and when he had ascended that he could look out upon the plaza through the apertures where the windows had been. Before him tumbled piles of brick, woodwork and old doors stretched the length of the floor and, as he stood there at the top of the ramp something moved, bits of brick or mortar trickled from a distant pile.

He waited a moment, then he drew his gun from its holster and started forward, and a moment later he almost blasted a huge gray rat into Kingdom Come; he was that jumpy.

The rat darted up an aisle between the rubble and vanished and he walked on until he came abreast of the aperture through which he thought the shot had been fired. From that spot alone the view of the corner building on the far side of the plaza was unobscured by trees.

And there was evidence. At the foot of a pile of bricks that stood a few yards inside the window opening a brass cartridge case glittered. Near it stood a slender bottle which had contained an orange drink and there was a greasy piece of brown paper stuck in among the bricks. That was what the rat had been after, he thought. He pulled the paper out and on it there were flakes of tortilla, sauce, bits of meat. Someone had waited there, eating a *taco* bought at a street stand, having a drink.

The cartridge case had contained a bullet made for a light sporting rifle. For a moment he stood holding it, gazing out over the plaza, past the Ferris wheel and the whirligig to that building on the corner; then he dropped the cylinder of brass into the pocket with the flashbulb and walked back to the ramp.

A block down from the plaza he found a cab. He gave the driver the address of the black-haired lady, the first one in his notebook, Rowena King, and as they started along the street he was aware of a shadow detaching itself from the crowd on the walk, and in a shop window across the street he saw the reflection of the car, saw the little boy standing on the bumper, bending forward, clinging leech-like to the trunk compartment.

The house Rowena King lived in was on the outskirts of the town. The cab stopped before tall blue gates set in a high wall topped with the jagged bottoms of broken beer bottles. As he got out and paid the driver, the boy slid around on the far side of the car and, as the car drove off, went walking casually up the street. It was the same boy who had ridden with him from *Quo Vadis* to the police station.

"Hey, you!" Johnny called.

The boy turned and stared at him. He was barefooted. He had on a pair of cotton trousers that had once been white and a faded lavender shirt, and he could have been ten or fourteen. His hair was shaggy, his eyes large and fierce, and he wouldn't weigh eighty pounds.

"Come here," Johnny told him.

The boy approached a few steps. "*Qué?*"

"How are you called?"

"Yo?"

"Yes, you."

The boy stuck out a hand. "Gimme peso."

Johnny reached in his pocket. "Tell me why you go places with me." He held out a peso bill and the boy snatched it.

"Go to hell," the boy said.

"That's not polite," Johnny told him.

But the little character had been going away even as he said it. There was an alley between the buildings across the street and he vanished there only to immediately reappear, grinning derisively. Then he was gone.

For a moment Johnny looked carefully up and down the street and after he rang the bell by the black-haired lady's gate, he gazed up at the roofs of the buildings across the street until the small door in one of the gates opened to frame the face and figure of an old gardener in a straw hat, holding a machete.

"La Señora King," Johnny told him. He stepped through the door and followed the gardener along the drive to the house, pausing at the threshold of yet another lovely open *sala*, or living room. Looking through the room he could see a little boy three or four years old splashing in the shallows of a swimming pool and a woman in a bathing suit was standing with a glass in her hand watching the child.

The woman turned her head and saw the gardener, who had removed his hat and was pointing at Johnny with it and, as the gardener clapped his hat back on his head and went away, she came across a strip of grass into the living room.

She was a black-haired woman, somewhere in her late forties, he guessed. She had a good figure and a good tan, but her face was as tough as an old prizefighter's, and when she spoke her voice was like that, deep and shattered and hard.

"Hello," she said. "What can I do for you?

"I would like to speak to Mrs. King," Johnny told her. He had a card ready and he handed it to her.

She studied the card, squinting, holding it up and away. "Oh," she said. "So you're the detective. She gazed at him. "I'd never have guessed it.

He smiled. "Now and then that's an asset, ma'am."

"I'm Mrs. King's mother," she said, "Mrs. Enright. She went over to an archway and called, "Rowena!

After a moment a voice replied impatiently, "*What*, mother?"

"That detective from San Francisco is here," her mother said.

There was a quick, soft sound of bare feet on tile then and Rowena King came through the arch tugging up the strapless bra of a white, two-piece bathing suit.

Unlike her mother, whose eyes were a pale, faded blue, hers were intensely dark. As Alonzo Mendoza had told him, there was fire in her and, indeed, she had magnificent equipment.

"His name's John Crouch," Mrs. Enright said, peering at the card again.

"*Church*," Johnny said.

"How do you do, Mr. Church, Rowena King said. "It's a terrible thing, isn't it? We're all just numb about it."

"Not me," said Mrs. Enright. She looked at Johnny. "Just *once* he had me to his house. The older they get the younger they like them. Isn't it true? She turned and went over to a bar table, where she slopped some gin into the glass she carried; then she poured tomato juice from a pitcher.

"Mother," Rowena King said, "wait till lunch at least before you get yourself all plastered."

"I am not all plastered," Mrs. Enright announced with dignity. She turned. "I am simply in a state to ponder life and death—and things." She lifted the Bloody Mary. "Cheers, Mr. Crouch."

"Church," Johnny said. "Cheers, ma'am." He gazed upon Rowena King. Her hair was caught back in a pony tail and she looked no more than sixteen. "I gather you know why I'm here," he told her. He couldn t help staring. She had so much of everything, and everything she had was good.

She nodded, watching him look at her. "Say—" she said. She touched her hair. "Did I forget my wig or my teeth maybe?"

He smiled. "No, ma'am. I was only thinking—you shine forth like a good deed in a naughty world. Excuse the eyes, please."

She laughed, her glance giving him a touch of heat, then she moved away, swung it, turned it, deposited it on a couch. She leaned back, gazed up at him from peach-colored cushions. "Get that ma'am stuff," she declared slowly. "Sit down, Mr. Church."

He sat down in a chair facing her, and there wasn't much to either top or bottom of the white suit; she was principally flesh, a wonderful advertisement for the pleasures thereof, a satiny, tanned, full-fashioned girl.

He gazed thoughtfully at her navel for a moment, then he said, "Mr. O'Dell's mother sent me down to find out what I can about his death. I've talked to Mr. Mendoza and I've talked to the police. The chief said he had questioned you ladies who were there at O'Dell's Saturday night."

"Yes," she said. "Chief Guiterrez and another one were here yesterday. I couldn't tell them anything but that I was there and that I came home when the others did. And that's about all I can tell you too."

He smiled at her, then he let her have it. "I figure you went back there Saturday night," he said.

His remark established a silence. In the silence the little boy in the pool began to bellow as a nursemaid lifted him from the water and wrapped him in a towel; and even there, he realized, the distant, frantic music of the carnival penetrated faintly.

"That's a hell of a remark to make!" the mother said deeply. She came over from the bar table and sat down in a chair. "What do you mean by that remark?"

"I'll stand on it," Johnny said, gazing at Rowena King. "What do you say, ma'am?"

She shook her head. "I'm not speaking to you."

"Damn you," the mother rumbled. "What do you mean coming here and—"

He cut her off. "A man was *murdered*" he told her, and the word had a sobering effect.

Mother and daughter exchanged a glance. "The police could have told you I didn't go back there," Rowena King said. "They checked my story."

"Will you tell me the story?"

She gazed at him broodingly a moment. "I guess," she said. "I really don't know why, except I'd like to see you swallow what you said."

"Listen," he told her, "that remark of mine was made for its shock value. I was trying to throw you off balance so I could take a look at you that way."

"How did I look?"

"Pretty level," he admitted.

"All right," she said. "I came home from O'Dell's. I let myself in."

"Anyone see you come in?"

"Mother," she told him. "The servants were in Tepoztlan."

That again, he thought.

"And—" she went on. "From about one o'clock until some time after two o'clock I was talking on the telephone. I was talking long distance to someone in Paris, Mr. Church."

"Paris, France," her mother said. "The man she's going to marry." She paused, then said, with her voice sliding ominously down the scale, "Maybe."

"The police called the phone company from this house yesterday and verified that call," Rowena King said.

"Then you went to bed, I guess," Johnny said.

"Then I went to bed."

"I bow my head, ma'am, in shame," he said.

"Have a drink!" the mother suggested.

He got up. "Thank you," he said. "I've got to go." He gazed at the girl, felt again the smouldering impact of those eyes. It would take a lot to distract her, he thought—even a murder wouldn't; she really had a one-track mind. "How do you get a taxi here when you want one?" he asked her.

"Phone," she said. She rose and crossed to a desk with a telephone on it. "*Ocho, nueve, tres,*" she said sweetly into the receiver. She was watching him. They could hear the carnival music again and she began to sway gently to it; she rolled her eyes.

"You've got a nice place here," Johnny told the mother.

"It ain't cheap," the mother growled. She gazed at her daughter. "Christ, he's older than I am, but what's the difference, so long as he's got it, Mr. Crouch? Don't you agree?"

"Church," he said.

"This is Señora King. I want a taxi. In a hurry!" She sang the word into the transmitter and put down the phone.

"Why do you always have to be getting into some damned jam!" her mother yelled.

Rowena said negligently, "Why can't you at least wait until lunch to get yourself stoned?"

"*I'm* the one that worries. That's why I get stoned! The only thing you ever worry about is who you're going to sleep with next!"

"What else is worth worrying over!" Rowena gave Johnny a dazzling smile, then she came and took his arm. "Come on," she said. "I'll escort you to the gate."

He said good-by to the mother and when he and Rowena King had gone a few steps along the drive the hand that was under his arm nudged him. "That's a gun, is it not?"

"Yes, ma'am," he told her.

"When do you stop saying 'ma'am?'"

"When I take off the gun."

"Boy," she said, "you're really all Sherlock, aren't you?"

"No," he said, "right at this moment I'm only about ten percent Sherlock."

"What's the other ninety percent?"

"That I'd rather not tell you on such short acquaintance," he said.

"Maybe we can prolong it."

"Sometime when I take the gun off," he said. They were at the gates then and when he opened the little door in the gate he saw the taxi waiting. He looked at her once more. "Go with God."

"Don't shoot yourself."

"What kind of a jam are you in?"

"Ah—" She stared at him and a flicker of concern or annoyance came and went in her eyes. "I had a fight over the phone with the guy who's in Paris," she said. She laughed softly, gazing at him. "He's *jealous*."

"I guess he doesn't have any reason to be, does he?"

"Oh, heavens *no.*" She dipped her lashes at him; and now she was moving the equipment again, rotating it gently to the strains of a distant rumba. "Stay for lunch?" she suggested.

He swallowed. "I am now starting my count," he advised her. "Ten, nine, eight, seven—"

"Dear old mater will pass out ere long."

"Six, five, four—" He hesitated. Everything now, even his pulse, had that tempo de rumba beat.

"There won't be anyone around."

"Three!" he said. "Two, *one!*" He slipped through the door and slammed it after him, and for a moment he leaned there against the blue gates, breathing deeply, gazing up into the blue, burning sky.

CHAPTER SIX

H E GAVE THE cab driver the address of the red-haired lady, Eleanor Staples, and this time no small, delinquent shadow rode the rear bumper.

"Where is your stand?" he asked the driver.

"At the foot of this hill and around the corner by the cantina, señor," the man said.

"Did the police question you?"

The driver glanced at him in the rear-view mirror. "The police? No, Señor. Why should they question me?"

"I am also police," Johnny told him. "*Un ojo privado.*" He grinned inwardly. "A private detective."

"Sí, *señor.*"

"I wish to know if the Señora King called for a cab from your stand on Sunday morning—yesterday. The hour would be some time between two and three o'clock."

"Sí *Señor.*"

"Do you have such knowledge yourself?"

"No, señor."

"Will you please find this out for me?"

"Sí, *señor,*" the driver said. "I can tell you this. She phoned for me only an hour or so ago."

"Where did you take her?"

"To the *casa de funeraria*, called *Quo Vadis*, señor. She stayed only a moment, then I drove her home."

Johnny pondered this information. Had all three gone to view the debonair corpse? If just one had *not* gone, there might be something in it.

The redhead's address led to a street that ran along the brink of one of the ravines that traversed that hilly town. The day was several points more humid down there by the ravine and the shrubs blossomed in tropical magnificence. Johnny gave the driver twenty pesos and asked him to phone him at his hotel. If he wasn't in he directed the man to leave a message. Then he rang the bell beside the gates, and there was a sign: "*Quinta Pomposa.*"

A maid admitted him and, as he had surmised from the sounds that came drifting over the wall, the *Quinta Pomposa* was a guest house, a horrendous one of too-red tile and too-white plaster, with floral designs painted on cane-bottomed chairs, a player piano and a television set going full blast.

Lunch was about to be served and drinks were being dispensed at a tiny bar, about which the jolly, pompous gray guests had gathered. They were, all of them, middle-aged to old, eyeglasses and bridgework glittering as they laughed at one another's remarks. He heard a man's voice shouting, "Hey, boy—tequila!" Then a woman's voice rising in a shrill, nasal whine, "Oh, now, *Cliff!*" Meanwhile, the player piano was tinkling out a John Sousa march, and a uranium blonde was breaking her heart over some lyrics on the TV.

He was glad to follow the maid out and along a path that wound among boxlike guest cottages and the only reason he could think of for anyone to be living there was that it would be cheap.

The maid stopped and pointed to one of the little tile-and-plaster boxes. The boxes had been given the names of flowers instead of numbers and the one Eleanor Staples lived in was called *Copa de Oro* in honor of the vine of that name which twined along the wrought-iron railing of the little porch.

The door to Cup of Gold was ajar and when he stepped onto the porch he saw two suitcases lying open on a bed and standing by the bed was a young lady in a candy-striped silk dressing gown. He stood there and watched her wrap a revolver in a lacy half-slip and tuck it away in one of the suitcases, then he knocked and she turned and looked at him with great, dark blue eyes. Her hair was a dark shade of red, almost chestnut colored and, though she had more mileage on her than Rowena King, she wasn't any bag.

Surprising her that way, he got a look at Eleanor Staples with her guard down and she looked, he thought, as if she had just lost her last quarter in a crooked slot machine; and, also, as if she might have gotten beaten up for complaining about it. There was a bruise on her right cheek and, despite an effort at camouflage, he could see that she had a black eye. Even with these disfigurements she was lovely.

That O'Dell—he thought. Had good taste. He pushed the door open. "You're Mrs. Staples?" She nodded and he held out his card. "My name's Church."

I don't need the card," she said. "Alonzo Mendoza told me about you." She had a beautiful voice, soft and Southern. She shook her head. "I'm afraid I can't tell you anything that might help you."

He smiled. "You could tell me who hit you."

"Nobody hit me," she said. She sat down abruptly and with a certain lack of coordination on the bed and the striped silk slid, revealing a pleasant expanse of rounded amber thigh, a display of which she appeared either unaware or considered of no possible interest to anyone.

"I fell," she told him. "When I came back here Saturday night I just got myself plain, stinkin' drunk, Mr. Church, and when I woke up I was lying on this floor."

She gazed at him, really looked at him now. She saw that he was male and breathing and did not have two heads. And now her self-display became a studied thing. She gave a token push at the striped silk, she thrust out her breasts and ran her fingers up through her cap of curls. The faint downy growth on her forearms, he noted, was the same reddish, chestnut color as her hair.

"Why did you want to get drunk?" he asked her.

"Because everything was over," she said.

"Between O'Dell and you?"

"Yes, Mr. Church."

He lowered himself into a cane-bottomed chair, which creaked plaintively beneath him, and as he did so she rose and he watched her cross to the bureau and pick up a bottle half-full of tequila.

"Drink, Mr. Church?"

"No, thanks."

She poured a man-sized portion of the liquor into a glass and tossed it off. "Ugh," she said. She shut her eyes.

"Mr. Mendoza said there was some talk of you marrying O'Dell."

"Everything was over," she repeated. "Kim was going away."

"So Mr. Mendoza said."

She was staring at her reflection now in the mirror above the dresser. "Oh, Alonzo—" she said. He's such a darlin' old grape. I'm going to miss him."

"Does Mr. Mendoza like the ladies?" he asked thoughtfully.

"Ho!" she exclaimed. "He's a regular old *satyr*, Mr. Church. If you know what I mean. Seems like he's always got a hand on your bottom somehow. Only with Alonzo you just don't mind it." She hiccuped, still gazing at herself. "I'm goin' to miss it all!" she whispered. "It was like a dream—that beautiful house, the beautiful parties. I would see myself livin' there." She laughed

VECHEL HOWARD

in a rather wistful, rather tipsy, way and reached for a crumpled package of cigarettes lying on the bureau. "I suppose some old Texas oil millionaire will buy it now," she said. She glanced at him. "You wouldn't happen to have an *American* cigarette, would you?"

"Yes, ma'am," he told her. He got out his cigarettes and lit one for her and his eyes met hers over the flame. "Mr. Mendoza said he was going to buy back O'Dell's house."

She moved over to the bed and sat down again. "That's Alonzo's grand delusion," she declared. "He just doesn't have the money any more, but he simply keeps forgetting that. Oh, he used to have it. They say half the people around here used to work for the Mendozas. Or, anyhow, their fathers and grandfathers did. Then came the revolutions, you know, and the land reforms."

"He seems to do all right," Johnny remarked. He got up. It was time to get to work.

"Oh, he's got an income," Eleanor Staples said. She crossed her legs, plucking absently once more at the sliding silk. "I don't think he even has to pay his servants. They're all scared to death of him—all the Indios are." She blew out smoke, gazing at him. "Habit, you know."

He took a step toward the bed and at first the blue eyes widened with interest, then they filled with dismay as he reached into the suitcase and took out the gun.

"Where did you get it?" he asked her. He tossed the lacy garments back into the suitcase.

"Kim O'Dell gave it to me," she said. "Sometimes I would be very late coming home—here—and, until the owner gave me a key, I would have to stand outside and wait for the porter to answer the bell."

He examined the gun. It was a .32 and there were five cartridges in the cylinder. He sniffed the gun barrel, sighted through it. If the gun had been fired recently it had been thoroughly cleaned.

"Did the police see this?" he asked her.

"No," she said. She stood up, put a hand on his arm. "You wouldn't make trouble for me, would you?"

"Not unless you've got it coming," he said.

She went over and poured herself another drink and tossed it off, then she came back over and put her arms around his neck. "I didn't do anything," she murmured. She ran a hand over his hair. "I didn't *do* anything, I don't know anything. Please—I don't want to get mixed up in a scandal. I've got my family back home to think about." She kissed his cheek, came gently in against him. "Just be nice to me."

He slipped the gun in his pocket, then he put his hands on her waist and sat her firmly on the bed. He gazed at her and said, "I guess you were jealous of O'Dell's other ladies, weren't you? That would be natural."

No, I wasn't, she said. "Kim never would have married one of them. They had no background. *My* mother was a Crabb, you know—and that means something. At least in Alabama, it does. Anyhow, I'm not just some mongrel nobody, like those other two. When Kim gave an important party he always asked *me* to act as hostess."

"I've got two more questions," he told her. "Number one—do you own a camera?"

"No," she said.

"Do you have any men friends here?"

"Only Alonzo now," she said.

"All right," he told her. He glanced at the bags. "Just don't leave town, lady."

She jumped up. "You haven't any authority over me! All I want to *do* is to get out of here!"

"If you run out," he said, "I'll turn the gun over to the police and they'll pick you up at the border."

"You wouldn't!" she wailed. Then her voice abruptly became soft and drawly again. "Would you *really* do that?"

"I sure as hell would," he said. "If another set of figures won't add up for me I'll have to give the gun to the police anyhow. In my book you could be it. Maybe I don't need to tell you, but the bullet that did for O'Dell came from a gun this size."

"I can't *afford* to stay here any longer," she said.

"You finish packing and take a taxi to the hotel on the plaza," he told her. "I'll pay your bill there." He walked over to the door. "Got it straight?" he asked her, turning back.

"I got it straight," she said bitterly. When she jumped up the gown flared. Now she arranged it more modestly. "I'll be seeing you, I presume." She gave him a slow, wet-lipped smile.

"Yes," he said. "You sure will." He turned then and went out.

The ladies were a hungry lot down there, even when in distress, he thought. Maybe it was the humidity, or the tequila. Anyhow, as he had suspected all along, there had been nothing beneath that dressing gown but Southern fried chicken.

In the now empty lobby of the main building, Johnny phoned for a cab. He waited inside the gates until the car came and after they got started he asked the driver if he had taken the red-haired American lady to or from the *quinta* on Saturday night. He hadn't. However, he knew the lady referred to and if the señor did not mind a slight delay he would stop at the stand where the two other drivers were now eating their lunch and he would ask them.

The stand was at a small bar-restaurant on the way to the plaza. The driver parked there behind the two other cabs and went in. When he came back out he said one driver had driven the red-haired lady to the house of the dead American, Señor Q'Dell, between eight and eight-thirty Saturday night. The other driver had taken her just an hour ago in the *casa de funeraria*, called *Quo Vadis*. He had waited there for her and driven her back to the *quinta*. Neither driver had taken her anywhere late Saturday night.

So, Johnny thought, maybe the lady had called a cab from some other stand. If she'd had homicide in mind she wouldn't have wanted to leave tracks.

CHAPTER SEVEN

ALL OVER TOWN a comparative quiet had fallen. There were no more explosions, most of the cabs were parked in shade and, though the merry-go-round and the Ferris wheel continued to turn and wheeze their mechanical music, the blare of the speaker had ceased. Even the one with the sporting rifle must have knocked off for lunch, Johnny thought.

There, was a message for him at the hotel desk saying Señor A. Mendoza had phoned. Mendoza left his number and requested Señor Church to call him back. And the clerk behind the desk was most respectful when he handed Johnny the message.

Clearly, as the redhead had said, the name of Alonzo Mendoza meant something in that town, the memory of a power descended from Cortez, a memory present everywhere—in the great cathedral that Cortez had built, in the pink palace, in the very air.

His room faced on the inner court of the hotel, where there were trees and grass and a swimming pool. The stairs were outside. Both the stairs and the balcony upon which the second-floor rooms opened were sheltered by a wide overhang of the tiled roof. His room was number 210, near the head of the stairs and, when he had unlocked the door and entered he flipped the window blinds shut. Then he got a razor blade from his shaving kit and he wrapped Eleanor Staples' .32 in a face towel. Next he made a slit in the cloth covering in the bottom of the box springs on one of the twin beds and wedged the gun in there between the springs.

That gun could be a hot item, he thought. If and when it looked like it might be the smart thing to make a little trouble for Chief of Police Guiterrez by asking him to test a bullet fired from it he wanted to be sure the gun was around.

He had just straightened from hiding the gun when his phone rang and it was the driver he had asked to check on Rowena King. The man had questioned the other drivers who used his stand, he said, and Señora King had not called for a cab at any time late Saturday night, or early Sunday morning.

Johnny set the phone down thoughtfully. Once more he thought of that bed of O'Dell's and the black hairs on the pillow. And now, with just the honey blonde left to talk to, he was puzzled.

He took off his jacket, unslung his gun and loosened his tie; then he phoned Mendoza. He spoke to a servant and a moment later Mendoza's ebullient voice came booming from the receiver.

"Señor Church!" the old gentleman exclaimed. "What progress?"

"Not much," Johnny told him.

"You haven't solved everything yet?"

"No," he said. "Did they get the safe open?"

Mendoza laughed gleefully. "Not yet. And, believe me, they are in a stew. The local locksmith has given up. Now they are phoning Mexico City for a specialist."

"I have spoken to two of the ladies," Johnny said.

"So I hear!"

"They called you?"

"Oh, yes indeed," Mendoza said. "They keep in very close touch with me. And now, hear this, my friend. Rowena and Eleanor are quite enchanted with you. Which brings me to the reason I called you a few minutes ago. I want you to dine with me this evening. Come at eight o'clock. The three ladies will be present, also Jervis and Irene, of course."

"Thank you for the invitation," Johnny told him. "I'll be there."

When he went back downstairs the dining room and the glassed-in terrace were filled with people eating. The headwaiter found him a small table on the terrace and he ordered lunch, deciding to have a rum and bitters first to sooth his ruffled libido. He really hoped now the blonde would turn out to be a quiet, unhungry type; another one like the other two, he thought, and he would be tempted to hang up his gun, settle for the cook's son as O'Dell's killer and proceed to enjoy himself. It would be so much simpler that way. Perhaps the police, taking the long view, were right. Why stir up trouble? Dead was dead, wasn't it?

When his drink arrived he drank to the ladies, the lovely leavings of O'Dell, who wanted no trouble, wanted only to be loved, cuddled and have their charms appreciated. Under the circumstances, it seemed a shame to snoop and pry, to suspect, harass and question.

The terrace was crowded with American tourists, the air was jumping with their talk, the inflections of the great Southwest and Midwest appearing to prevail. At a table adjacent to him the Southwest was represented by two couples, and clearly this foursome had not just descended from a tourist limousine, a bus or private car for a lunch stop in the town; they were staying there. Their waiter knew them—indeed, their needs claimed his entire attention—and now and then one of them would favor the gauche and noisy transients with a stony look of disdain. The men were lean and weather-beaten and so were their wives, but by the number and size of the ladies' diamonds and by the talk he overheard Johnny deduced that these were not just some simple farm folk on a Mexican holiday.

A man approached their table. "Gentlemen," he greeted the two men. He bowed and one of the men introduced him to the ladies as Mr. Gallatin.

Mr. Gallatin was a tall and handsome man with graying hair and a sardonic but amiable expression. "You fellows licking your wounds?" he inquired.

"Was we hurt?" one of the men drawled to the other.

"I didn't feel nothin'," the other said.

"Well, any time you want a chance to get even—" Gallatin suggested. "I'm available." He smiled, winked at the ladies and walked across the terrace into the hotel lobby.

"Ain't he nice *lookin*'," one of the women said.

The men glanced at each other. "I don't say he cheats," one of them remarked after a moment. "When I say that about a man I'll have my proof an' a six-gun handy. I just say I don't aim to set down to no pokah table with that fella again."

The foursome rose, the men threw bills carelessly on the cloth and they moved toward the street. And at that moment Johnny noticed the dark, fierce little face pressed against the terrace glass.

It was his shadow again.

The boy's eyes followed the departing foursome, rested momentarily on the bills they had thrown down, then returned to Johnny. When he saw that Johnny was watching him he slipped on along the glass, ducked around a parked car and lost himself among the clotted, slowly moving figures in the plaza.

His waiter told him how to get to the hotel the blonde lady, Helen Wellington, lived in. The hotel was up the little street at the west side of the plaza, the waiter said.

When he left the terrace the shutters of some of the shops were still closed for the midday break and people were still eating and napping beneath the old trees in the plaza. He bought a bag of peanuts from a vendor and for a while he stood watching the merry-go-round. When he went on he saw his shadow once more. The boy was standing in front of a booth that sold carnival dolls, giant antic mice and great fuzzy white rabbits and teddy-bears with ribbons around their necks.

For a moment Johnny thought the boy was going to buy something at the booth; he saw him get his money out and count it and for a moment he looked as if he were getting up his nerve to speak to the man behind the counter; then the Ferris wheel gave a last discordant wheeze of doubtful melody and as the great wheel slowed the boy turned, rushed over and bought a ticket; and he was in such a high state of anticipation and en chantment as he stood there waiting in line to get on the wheel that he didn't notice Johnny when he bought a ticket and went to stand in line behind him.

People got off, others took their places and when the boy slid into the last vacant seat Johnny was right behind him. The attendant fastened the bar in front of them, music blared forth once more and the seat lurched upward to soar above the laurel trees into the sky.

He watched the boy's face, saw him gaze down wide-eyed, gripping the bar, saw him pale as the seat swayed over the top of the great circle. As they started down the boy turned to him, a grin of delight on his face.

"Great, isn't it!" Johnny said. "Have a peanut." He put the bag in the boy's lap.

The grin had frozen. At first Johnny thought the boy might try to jump out, then it was as if a pin had been stuck in him, releasing all his fierceness. He shrank back into a corner of the seat, deflated, scared.

"You don't have to be afraid of me," Johnny told him as they returned to the sky. He let the wheel make a full turn before he spoke again. "How are you called?"

The kid flashed a glance at him. "Tomas, Señor," he whispered after a moment. He took a peanut from the bag, his face taut and excited as they soared over the top again.

"Why do you follow me?" Johnny asked after a moment, but the boy did not reply. The question scared him and once more he shrank back into his shell.

From the Ferris wheel the panorama of the plaza, with its adjacent streets and buildings, appeared as if in kaleidoscope, flashing upon the screen of vision as the seat topped the trees, vanishing as the seat once more swooped earthward. And, at one of those aerial apexes just before the ride ended, Johnny, glancing absently beyond aboreal greenery, saw in the tourist station across the street a man who made him forget the boy beside him, the ladies, the late O'Dell and everything else. And as the seat zoomed down once more, then slowed abruptly there was a sick, sinking sensation in his stomach that was not due only to the abrupt alteration in gravity.

Once more the wheel chugged slowly aloft and they hung swaying above the trees while passengers were disembarked below, and once more he could see across the street. One of the *tourismo* cars, the beat-up old seven-passenger jobs that made the trip to and from Mexico City, had just pulled into the station and several passengers were standing around waiting for the driver to take their luggage from the trunk, but the man upon whom Johnny's eyes were fastened had his luggage; it was one of those little zipper bags some of the airlines issued.

The man was the Banker; no doubt of it, Johnny thought. The face, with its neat black mustache, was still Chicago pale, unchanged by Las Vegas sun, and he had the limp. The Banker was tired from his trip and the limp was pronounced as he came from the station and turned down toward the plaza hotel.

Again the wheel chugged, then stopped with their seat resting on the platform. The bar was lifted and Johnny caught the arm of the boy Tomas, as he tried to run. He pressed peso bills into a small, dirty brown hand. "Here," he said. "Buy stuff. Have fun."

He strolled back the way he had come, paused by the doll booth and now the Banker, a slight man in a dark silk suit and a cocoanut-straw snapbrim hat, was crossing the narrow street that led up to the market. Church bells began tolling and Tomas' voice could be heard over at the booth: Johnny glanced over, saw the boy with a rabbit, heard him complaining because one of the rabbit's ears would not stand up, haggling with the keeper of the booth. Meanwhile, the Banker moved on and entered the hotel. Johnny turned away then, started walking toward the west side of the plaza.

What was the Banker doing there?

He was called the Banker, some said, because of the way he dressed, always neat and conservative, always looking grave and dignified. He was also cold, hard and untouchable. Others said he had gotten his nickname because in his youth he had banked a poker game in a South Side speakeasy. That was in Chicago before he came west. He was also known as Benny the Banker and Benny Ruggio, which was really his right name.

When Johnny Church had been with the Gerard Agency in Chicago he had sometimes, in the line of duty on a case, gone to a nightclub there that the Banker owned a piece of. The Banker was a gambler, but not a big one, and the pieces he owned of things were always little pieces. First and foremost, Benny Ruggio was a rub-out artist. That was what he was known for, handsomely paid for. When you saw the Banker or heard his name what you thought of were bullet-ridden bodies, and no clue to the killer.

The day was no longer bright and beautiful. It was as if a wind right off the glittering white peak of Popocatepetl had just swept the town. Death, in a silk suit, had just passed and the music of the wheel and the merry-go-round now sounded strictly like a dirge. Johnny thought of *Quo Vadis*. Could it be that the Banker had come there for *him*? Was he the one who had overdrawn on life?

CHAPTER EIGHT

T HE BLONDE'S HOTEL was small, old and beautiful. He passed
through a great stone arch, where grilled-iron Spanish gates
would be closed and locked at night, then he crossed an expanse
of mosaic tile to the registration desk. Flanking the entry were a
small bar and a dining room.

"La Señora Wellington, he told the clerk.

The clerk sat down at the switchboard and stuck in a plug.
"Who shall I say is calling, *por favor*, señor?"

"Señor Church."

The clerk spoke to the lady and hung up. She asks that you
please wait a few minutes, señor. Then go up. It is room ten, up
the stairs and straight ahead." The switchboard buzzed and the
clerk plugged in again. "*Sí, señora.*"

Johnny strolled back to the archway and lit a cigarette. He
leaned against the stone, smoking, and when he finished the cigarette he crossed the mosaic once more, climbed the stairs and
went along a wide, cool hall to number 10.

Having encountered those two amoral samples of O'Dell's
taste in the ladies, he did not expect to have one with skinned-
back hair and spectacles open that door and start singing hymns,
and yet nothing could have quite prepared him for the girl who
did open the door. It was the one he had seen come into the hotel
as he ate breakfast that morning. It was, for an instant, his Laura
come to life once more. Then, almost at once, it was not; it was
a girl with a beauty and a character that were her very own, a

lovely, vibrant-looking, honey blonde, gray eyes sparkling into his own, brows arched, a quizzical smile on her lips.

"Wellington?" At the moment, it was all he could say.

"Wellington," she agreed. "You're Church." She stepped aside, holding the door wide open for him. She was wearing a brief robe of white cotton piped in red, with a red zipper on it that wound a serpentine track down her front. She had on red sandals and red earrings, and her lips and fingernails, of course, were also red. She was all poetry, he thought—exotic, erotic—in red, in white, her skin all tanned and velvety-looking.

After he stepped past her he turned at once to look at her again, not wanting to take his eyes off her. And he thought: Oh, lady, be cold, hey? Be nasty.

It was a large room opening on a balcony that over-looked a patio. Helen Wellington shut the door, then she moved slowly over to him, took his hand and led him out onto the balcony. She indicated a chair for him and, still holding him mesmerized and speechless with those great, urgent gray eyes, she sat, swung her legs up with a stunning display, and lay back on a chaise facing him.

If the other ladies had been hungry, he thought, this one was starving to death right before his eyes. Even the lavender shade they sat in became suddenly an aphrodisiac.

Start asking her some questions, he told himself. Talk. And for a while you better keep those big dumb brown eyes of yours elsewhere.

"I have talked to the two other ladies who were present at O'Dell's Saturday night," he said. He stared out at the top of a banana tree in the patio.

"Oh, I know that!" she told him. "I know every question you asked them, *everything*. They both phoned Alonzo the instant you left."

"Everything funnels into Mendoza, it seems."

"And *out*," she declared. "You're going to ask me if I went back to O'Dell's that night, aren't you?"

"And you're going to tell me 'No,'" he said.

She laughed, soft, golden notes that hung above them for an instant. "Yes," she said.

He gazed at her and her brows and her long lashes were black. "Will you tell me a little bit about yourself, ma'am?" he asked her. "How did you happen to come here? And how did you meet O'Dell?"

"I'm from Dayton, Ohio," she said. "I went out to Las Vegas last spring to get a divorce. I stayed at the same place O'Dell's second wife—the one before Irene—was staying, and when she heard I was thinking of making a trip down here she told me to be sure and look up Kim O'Dell. She's been married and divorced twice now since she left him."

"Was your ex-husband, Mr. Wellington, a wealthy man?" he asked her.

"J. Stuart Wellington wasn't and isn't hurting," she declared.

"Did he do all right by you?"

"After my lawyers twisted his old arms almost off and stuck pins in him for a while he did make a modest settlement to compensate me for the two years of unadulterated boredom I spent as his wife."

"He was an older man?"

"Yes," she said. "In *every* way."

"You prefer older men, ma'am?"

"Only if they're fun," she said. "Fun in every way."

"O'Dell was fun?"

"Oh, yes. He was fun."

He shook his head slowly. "Always leave 'em laughing," he said. "Even if it kills you."

"Kim wouldn't have wanted it any other way," she told him. "That's how he was. And that's the kind of men I like—the kind that just won't take life, death or themselves too seriously. Kim wouldn't have wanted anyone to weep for him."

He gazed at her and by now the initial shock of her affect upon him had worn off enough to permit him to do a little thinking. If Rowena really hadn't gone back there that night, he thought, then this one had to qualify.

"Well," he told her, "you talked to the police. Maybe they checked on what you did after you left O'Dell's, maybe they didn't. Anyhow, the old lady up there in San Francisco who hired me isn't laughing. My agency is collecting money from her to find out who killed her son. That's what I'm getting paid for, and I want to tell you I'll check on you, ma'am. So, if you did go back there to O'Dell's Saturday night, it will be less sweat for everybody if you'll just tell me the truth right now. I'm not down here to investigate the moral climate of the American colony, you know. I mean you don't have to by shy with me. I've been around."

"I'm not shy," she said. "And I think I like you, Church."

She made that last remark slowly and with a lot of feeling, so much feeling it scared him. She was, it seemed, even less inhibited than the other two ladies and, on top of that, she had a force and drive the other two didn't have. This one, he felt, would always do just what she damn well pleased—and, watch out, *don't* get in her way.

She moved those velvety limbs on the chaise once more and he rose abruptly to his feet. All right, he thought, after all, it's *business*. There's an investigation to be made. Besides, if I don't, I'll kill myself some day when I think of what I missed.

"I'd like to run a little personal check on you now," he told her. "Would you step inside, please, ma'am." He stood there, meeting her eyes, watching her get up off the chaise.

"What kind of a little personal check?" she asked interestedly when they faced each other in her room.

For answer he took her in his arms and met those lips of hers with his. And right away it was as if he had stuck a finger in a light socket. She responded then, jolting him, engulfing him, her fingers digging trenches in his back.

Finally, to break it for a minute, he had to push her away so that she staggered a bit; they were standing near the bed. He wiped his lips carefully with a clean handkerchief and looked at the stain the lipstick made, but it was nothing conclusive. Meanwhile, there had been a noise behind him and the light abruptly failed as draperies went slithering across the French doors. When he turned he saw her standing there magnificently nude, eyes smoky, breathing like a tigress, with the cotton robe lying at her feet. And when he moved toward her it was with the certain knowledge that the search for the lady who had been in O'Dell's bed Saturday night had *not* been narrowed down to Rowena King.

The speaker in the plaza was blaring again, and intermittently, Johnny could hear the music of the merry-go-round and the Ferris wheel. He lay on his back in the dusky room and smoked a cigarette and her pretty fingers were tracing patterns on his chest.

"Who was it I remind you of?" she asked in a soft, warm voice.

"Don't know," he said. "Do you still say you came right back here Saturday night?"

"Yes," she said. "You told me I reminded you of somebody a while ago. Remember?"

"The girl," he said finally, "was my wife."

"Where is she now?"

"Dead," he said.

They had been married in New York, he and Laura, gone to Miami on their honeymoon; then he had been transferred to the office in Kansas City.

A rich and proud family had a son who had fallen in with bad company, a bop, gone crowd, maybe taking dope, and they wanted to find out. The agency had put him on the case and he had turned up a pusher, and in working back on that one he'd bumped into a big bad dog who had told him to lay off or for him it would be a concrete nightie and the river. But it had not been him they got. It had been Laura. When she went out to the delicatessen one Sunday morning, they had run her down with a big black car. And what Johnny had done to the one who was behind it hadn't made him a very pretty corpse.

That had been the last of Kansas City for him. For a while it had been the last of everything.

Right now, it reminded him of the Banker, and that was enough to ruin anybody's day. He rolled out then, left that splendid, tireless lady in her hay and, while she looked on lovingly, he began to dress.

They wouldn't, or they couldn't, tell him anything—none of them. Or, if they had, he thought, he didn't know it yet.

CHAPTER NINE

MENDOZA'S MAN let him in. His *patrón*, he told Johnny, was at O'Dell's. There were sounds of hammering coming from O'Dell's, sounds of steel biting into brick and mortar, and the man explained that they were cutting a hole in the wall of Señor O'Dell's bedroom so that the expert from Mexico City could get at the back of the safe. The man would drill a small hole in the back of the safe, then he would insert a rod through the hole and unlock the lock.

"I wish to visit the nearest taxi stand," Johnny said. "Can you direct me?"

"Do me the favor, señor, to come with me," the man said. He led Johnny into the rear court and an old woman was sitting there at the top of a dark stone stair that led down beneath the house. She had two buckets and was plucking quail. Mendoza's man unlocked the door that opened on the little side street, that rear entrance common to the two houses and to which O'Dell's ladies had been given keys.

"Down this little street and around the corner to your left," the man said. "The telephone is in the *cantina* and the drivers park there outside."

"That is the stand that one would phone from Señor O'Dell's?"

"Yes, señor."

He saw the girl as the door shut behind him. She was coming up the narrow street and had obviously been to the carnival;

she was carrying one of the big white rabbits and she also had a pennant on a bamboo cane. VIVA MORELOS, the pennant said. She was wearing a low-cut white blouse, a figured cotton skirt and sandals and she was very beautiful; even with clothes on. It was the girl he had seen serving Alonzo Mendoza his fruit that morning.

He greeted her with a big smile, stood blocking her way. "*Buenas tardes, señorita*," he said. "Aren't you a little old to be playing with dolls?"

Her black lashes fell on her golden cheeks. She gazed at her feet. "It was bought for me, señor," she said.

"Your sweetheart bought it for you, perhaps?"

"Perhaps," she said. Her eyes flashed up at him.

"I saw you this morning," he reminded her. "Remember me?" She blushed. "*Sí, señor!*"

"I have never begun a day so pleasantly," he told her. "I think I shall come and visit your *patrón* each morning.

"Yes?" She stifled a laugh, sucked in her breath, and her young, unstayed breasts were high and firm beneath the light cotton blouse.

"How are you called?" he asked softly.

"Angelita, señor."

"I myself am called Juan," he said. "I think your name is beautiful."

"*Gracias, señor.*"

"Do you serve your *patrón* at night also?"

Her eyes flashed up at him again, read his meaning and once more color flooded her cheeks. She was startled, he could see—even rather scared by his question. "I am Indio, señor," she explained. "Only a peasant." She was trying to convey to him the vast gulf between humble people like herself and her noble *patrón*.

"I understand," he told her. "In the morning, then, Angelita!"
He stepped aside for her to pass, bowed low to her youth and
beauty.

"With your permission, señor!" She ran up to the door and
pressed the bell. She stood there snuggling the rabbit against her
cheek, darting little glances at him from the corners of her eyes
while she waited for the door to be opened. Then, as the door
was opened, she gave him a dazzling smile, whirled, her full skirt
swirling up about her golden legs, and, with a saucy switch of her
plump behind, she vanished.

There were two cabs parked around the corner at the foot of the
little street and the driver of the first car was sitting behind the
wheel, reading a newspaper. "*Sí, señor,*" he said, when Johnny
leaned in the window and questioned him. Three cabs from that
stand, he said, had picked up three ladies at Señor O'Dell's gate
about ten minutes after twelve Saturday night. Because so many
people were in Tepoztlan at the festival that night there had been
little business, so the three cars that used that stand had all happened to be there when the call from La Casa O'Dell came. He
himself had driven one lady to the hotel on the plaza.

Johnny frowned. "Can you tell me the color of the lady's
hair?"

The driver thought a moment, then shook his head. The evening had been misty and damp, he explained, and all three ladies
had worn their shawls over their heads.

The driver of the other car was in the *cantina* and that one
said when they went in to talk to him that he had taken the lady he
picked up at O'Dell's on Saturday night to the *Quinta Pomposa*.

The man who had driven the third cab was not working that
day. His wife had telephoned and said he was home drunk.

"Take me to him," Johnny told the first driver and they went out and got in the car.

They inched along narrow, cobbled streets past outdoor markets, past sad little stores and *cantinas* and finally stopped before the yawning black rectangle of a doorway in a pink plaster façade. They went in there and the driver, with many elegant phrases to the soiled, barefoot woman with a flower in her hair, asked for the driver called Manuel. A curtain was pulled aside, letting light into the black hole of an alcove where there was a bed and, as startled cockroaches scurried for cracks in the walls, the driver called Manuel, who lay fully clothed upon the bed, opened his eyes and shouted: "*Bola mala!*" He sat up, with his eyes crossed, his hair standing on end and again he shouted it—"Bad ball!"

Johnny's driver snickered. "Manuel umpires at the baseball games on Sunday," he explained. "It is a great strain on him because it is so hard for him to please everybody and after the game is over he always gets drunk." He turned to the man on the bed. "Stop calling those malodorous balls," he told him. "This gentleman has a question to ask you."

Johnny took out some money and laid it on the bed and the one called Manuel shook his head in pain for a moment and finally uncrossed his eyes. His eyes came to rest, with some evidence of attention, on Johnny.

"*Sí, señor?*" he said.

Speaking slowly and carefully Johnny asked him if he remembered where he had taken the lady he picked up at O'Dell's on Saturday night. The man nodded. He glanced at the other driver and with one forefinger he traced a circle in the air.

"Around the block," Johnny's driver said.

"To the back door of the Casa Mendoza," the one called Manuel said.

"That lady's hair—" Johnny gazed at him intently. "Did you notice the color of her hair?"

The man thought a moment and shook his head. He shrugged. "At night all cats are gray," he declared, and he flopped back on the bed.

CHAPTER TEN

IT OCCURRED to him that he wasn't making much progress. And it was the blonde who had helped to complicate matters, bless her. On the return ride to the hotel he was aware of that flashbulb rubbing against the cartridge case in his pocket; and, with a chill, he thought of the Banker. He pondered over the .32 he had taken from the redhead, and the shadowing kid. And he wondered where everything fit.

Maybe the police were right, he decided. Why knock yourself out? Dead was dead. Just say the cook's son did it and let it go at that.

One thing had been established—neither Rowena King nor Helen Wellington had told him the truth. Neither had returned directly to her own residence Saturday night. Hadn't the redhead perhaps made a *point* of being driven directly to her *quinta?*

When he stopped at the hotel desk to get his key he asked if Señora Staples had registered, and she had. The red-haired lady had been lodged in 108, a room on the ground floor beneath his own. He got his key and went up to his room and as soon as he entered he knew that he had had a visitor. He could tell by the picture, now slightly askew on the wall, by bureau drawers which had not been completely shut after being opened. He looked through his briefcase first and there was no news there, nothing disturbed. Next, he went over and reached up under the bed where he had hidden the redhead's gun. He felt among the springs, but the gun and the towel it had been wrapped in were gone.

A moment later he was on his way down the stairs once more. He walked along to room number 108, listened a moment, then tried the knob. The door opened and he stepped inside.

The brilliant afternoon light had softened, evening was on the way and the room was rosy with sunset and dusk. In that light the redhead's splendid amber body glowed with a chaste and exciting beauty. She was lying deep in sleep in the middle of the double bed, cuddling a pillow against her, looking helpless and childlike and lonely.

After a moment he crossed to the bed and pulled the sheet up over her so that he would not be distracted while he made his search. When he had finished in the bedroom he went into the bath. He looked in the toilet tank and the cabinet over the wash-bowl and after that there was nowhere else to look. For a moment he stood gazing at the towel rack, at the two clean face towels, the two bath towels, then he returned to the bedroom and phoned the bar, ordered a rum on the rocks for himself and a tequila sour for the lady.

When the boy came with the drinks he asked him where he could find the maid and the boy said the afternoon maid would be coming around soon to fill the water pitchers and check the rooms.

When he shut the door and turned he saw that Eleanor Staples was awake. She sat up, rubbed at her curls and groaned, and that amber torso rising from the snowy white swirl of the sheet, her breasts moving gently as she massaged her head, her slender waist, and full hips were the loveliest sight he had ever seen.

The ladies, he thought—God bless them. How dull life would be without them. He went over and handed her drink to her. "What did you do with the gun?" he asked.

"Angel," she whispered deeply. She took a long sip from the glass, and her eyes in that light were gentian-colored. She swallowed. "What did you say?"

He sat down in the chair by the bed and lit a cigarette and when she reached for it he handed it to her and lit another for himself. "Someone came into my room while I was out this afternoon," he told her. "They took that gun I took from you."

"Why would they want to do that?"

"I can think why you would," he said. He took a sip of his rum, watching her face.

"Honey," she told him, "I wish you'd get it out of your sweet, bristly little head that maybe I killed Kim O'Dell with that gun."

"Maybe you didn't," he said. "Maybe you just know who did."

"Honey, I *don't* know," she said. "I don't know any more than I told you before."

"You told Mendoza I took your gun, of course."

"Wasn't I supposed to?"

"And so, of course, the other ladies would know about it," he said, now thinking aloud. "Maybe a lot of other people too." He gazed at her. "Right now, though, it makes no sense to me for anybody else to take that gun but you." He paused. "Or—somebody you know."

"I don't know anybody," she declared. "Just practically nobody."

"Or," he continued, "somebody is playing games."

They finished their drinks and he phoned for another round; then, when the drinks were delivered, he sat there in the dusk thinking; and she lay, propped up on one elbow, letting him think, sipping and smoking, the great gentian eyes resting with a fond intentness on his face.

Presently the maid came. She checked the bathroom to see if soap or clean towels were needed and she filled the water pitcher on the bedside table and when she went out he followed her.

"How many face towels do you give to each room?" he asked her.

"Two for each person, señor," she said.

"I am Mr. Church in 210," he told her. "If you find an extra face towel in one of the rooms I want you to tell me which room you find it in."

He watched her nod, looking quite puzzled, and he winked at her, implying it was all part of some joke, and when he handed her the twenty-peso bill she smiled and repeated his name, then he climbed the stairs to his room, stripped off his clothes and got under the shower.

Between the time he came out of the shower and the time he got dressed again his phone rang three times. The first time it was Eleanor. She wanted to know why he just walked out like that without even a "See you later." And would he please pick her up on his way to Alonzo Mendoza's dinner party? He said he would.

The next call was from the black-haired Rowena, who wanted to know if she couldn't stop and pick him up on her way to Alonzo Mendoza's dinner party and when he said he had already promised to take a lady there she slammed down the phone.

The third call was from the blonde, Helen. "Lover," she said, "come on over."

"I can't at the moment," he told her. "Besides, you lied."

There was a pause; then she asked him, "What do you mean?"

He crossed his fingers for luck. "You told me you went right back to your room after you left O'Dell's Saturday night."

"Who told you any different?" she asked.

"A taxi driver. He told me he brought you to this hotel I'm in right now."

"I got off there to buy some American cigarettes," she said. "Look, lover—pick me up on your way to Alonzo's."

"I can't," he said. "I'm taking another lady there."

"You bastard," she murmured. "Just wait till I see you." She hung up.

Well, he thought as he put down the phone, it worked. Now I've completed a full circle. He had figured in the first place—and for more reasons than the obvious one—that Rowena King was the lady who had been in O'Dell's bed. And now, finally, he was sure of it.

CHAPTER ELEVEN

LEANOR HAD ON a strapless white gown and she wore a soft white shawl over her lovely shoulders. She carried a large white bag which she opened so that Johnny could see the bottle in it.

"You won't get a drink at Alonzo's," she declared. "Just let me know when you get thirsty, honey."

They were ushered into Mendoza's court by the porter and the big birds tethered in the surrealistic trees screamed at them. The other guests were in the great living room—Rowena in a peach-colored sheath of velvet, Helen in clinging satin cream.

Irene Maybrick, a glittering column of bottle-green taffeta, was with Jervis Ross. Both he and Mendoza were in dinner jackets, Ross in a white one, Mendoza's pink, an assemblage quite as dazzling and splendid as anything Johnny had ever seen in technicolor. For a moment, he simply stood there in his old tweed jacket and wrinkled pants admiring them.

The redhead gasped. "Drinks!" she cried.

There were, indeed, bottles of spirits of many varieties on a buffet table, with the man in the colored vest to serve, and everyone present but Mendoza held a glass.

"Eleanor, darling!" the old satyr exclaimed, hastening forward to greet the lady. "How splendid you look." He kissed her, then he grinned at Johnny. "Isn't she *lovely*?" He waved him toward the bar. "Now do get your horrible drinks quickly," he said. "Poison yourselves, drug your finer instincts! At any rate, please make all possible haste, as I wish to propose a toast to begin this wonderful evening." He clapped his hands sharply together. "Now don't any of you take a sip yet!" he commanded them. "Wait!" So saying he escorted, or rather propelled, Eleanor—who certainly required no extra urging to move in that direction— toward the bar and, meanwhile, Johnny noticed that the fine old hands really did get around, fluttering like butterflies about the lady's magnificent *derrière*.

The redhead and he got their drinks, then the barman put ice in a glass, poured soda over the ice, added a twist of lemon peel and handed the glass to Mendoza.

"Ladies and gentlemen," Mendoza announced, lifting the glass high, I give you Kim O'Dell!"

Everyone drank very promptly, not so much in O'Dell's honor, Johnny felt, as simply because they were tired of waiting and damn well wanted a drink; the minor anesthetic also helped to reduce the effect of Mendoza, who appeared that evening to be fizzing like a cannon-cracker fuse.

"It's Kim's liquor you're drinking," Mendoza informed them. "It was so thoughtful of him to leave me his cellar, and tonight I have made a breach in my legacy."

"Well," drawled the redhead, handing her empty glass to the barman, "'once more into the breach, dear friends.'"

"And tonight," Mendoza went on, "it is our dear, departed Kim, himself, who shall be our guest of honor." He clapped his hands again and, at the sound, an area of soft blue light appeared on the terrace beside the pool and in the light there was a five-piece marimba band which began at once with a sprightly Latin vigor to play *Danny Boy*.

"Oh, my God," Irene Maybrick groaned.

"That was one of Kim's favorite melodies!" Mendoza exclaimed to Johnny. "It's as if I can hear him singing it now. Isn't it sentimental? Isn't it touching?"

Johnny nodded. "I'm all choked up," he declared.

"That's enough *drinking!*" Mendoza called out above the music. "I simply won't have you all stupifying your taste buds with cocktails so that you won't appreciate my food. Now let us be seated! Never fear—there shall be wines!"

The redhead took Johnny's arm, Irene, rolling her eyes heavenward, took Ross's, and they followed Mendoza, who had flung an arm about each of the other two ladies, out onto the terrace and there they beheld a table where silver and crystal gleamed in candlelight. The chair at the head of the table facing them was banked with flowers and among the flowers, at the proper height for a head to be, there was a large photograph of O'Dell, his jolly, life-sized face beaming drolly at them all.

"*Alonzo!*" Irene cried. She gasped. "Oh, no, really—this is too ghastly. This is just too utterly macabre!"

"I quite agree," Jervis Ross said. "I can't sit down to dinner with him staring at me like that."

"Oh, *tut!*" Mendoza chided them. "Why not? What's wrong with you people? One would think you had never really known Kim O'Dell. Kim would have adored all this!"

The other ladies thought so too and Mendoza, his hands fluttering busily, seated his curvesome pair on either side of the place that had been laid for O'Dell, where an untouched Martini also waited. "You see," he told everybody, "if Kim weren't here, we would be shy a man. Now the sexes are in balance."

"I'm afraid I've lost my appetite," Irene Maybrick announced.

"Oh, you're always losing things!" Mendoza told her gaily. "Husbands, *bonds*—" He held out a chair for her and she abruptly sat in it; then Jervis Ross also seated himself.

"Did you get the safe open yet?" Johnny asked Ross.

"No," Ross said sourly. "The man broke a drill. He went off to get another one, and it wouldn't surprise me if he never came back. That's the way it is down here—they start something, a building or something, then they get tired of it. Did you ever see so many unfinished buildings?"

"You two made a terrible mistake," Mendoza told Ross and Irene, "in not going to see him at *Quo Vadis*." He appealed to the three lovely ladies. "Didn't he look splendid?"

"Marvelous!" the ladies chorused.

"After you left," Mendoza said to Johnny, "each of them came, and each of them kissed him. They left their three *beautiful* scarlet marks." He tapped his forehead. "Right here."

It was a dinner that Johnny Church was never going to forget—from the jellied terrapin to the Napoleon brandy. And, supplementing the many courses, were superb and gentle vintages from the cellar of O'Dell. And there was O'Dell, himself—his essence, his ghost—flavoring everything with his vanished personality. Like the others, O'Dell was served, his untouched plates removed, glasses of his wine were poured for him and Alonzo Mendoza, sipping soda water and nibbling daintily while he laced the evening with a constant fizz of talk, often addressed himself directly to O'Dell.

"Kim," Mendoza would say, "just as soon as I decided to have this party today I sent my hunter out to bag some quail. And I had the cook roast them with the tangerines in them, just the way you like." Or "This lobster!" he would exclaim to the photograph and flowers. "Isn't it better than thermidor? It's a dish I invented especially for this party!"

And, meanwhile, the marimba band kept playing Irish ballads that tended to sound like the rumbas and the old *ranchero* numbers they usually played, and the candlelight fell with soft reverence on the beautiful faces of O'Dell's three ladies, flickered on their shoulders, their hair. The candles lit little flames in the black-haired lady's eyes when she would look at Johnny, made the blonde's smoky eyes glow; the blonde would glance at him fiercely, her little pink tongue would slide along her upper lip and she would bare her white teeth so that the dimple showed in her right cheek, while beneath the table the redhead kept sliding a knee against one of his own.

And then there was Angelita, in a maid's uniform, with a masklike expression, helping the rest of Mendoza's staff to serve. He would wink at Little Angel whenever he could catch her eye, see mirth tug at the set line of her pretty mouth and he would gently pinch her saucy little bottom when she would take his plate away.

And, when he drank the vintages, he drank to O'Dell, the one who had made all this possible; for he knew he had never had it, probably never again would have it, quite so superlatively good.

With the brandy and the *café espresso*, a box of O'Dell's special brand of Havanas was opened and set at O'Dell's place and the musicians, happily, plunged into a samba. It was time now for dancing, Mendoza announced; the odd lady would dance with O'Dell.

Since Mendoza first requested the pleasure of a dance with Irene Maybrick, Ross asked the black-haired lady on his left, the redhead pulled Johnny to his feet and that left the blonde to dance with the ghost, and the lady rose nobly to the occasion. Hips undulating to the beat of the music, she smiled fetchingly up into a non-existent face, allowed spectral hands to twirl her. She laughed at unspoken witticisms, returned unwhispered whispers and altogether turned in such a fine, imaginative performance that everybody, even the musicians, got into the spirit of the thing and, when the black-haired lady's turn came, she was even better and the redhead was the best of all.

He had just begun to dance with Rowena King when, remotely, there was the sound of an electric drill and he saw Ross and Irene exchange glances. Work had been resumed on the safe.

"I've got to talk to you," Rowena King said.

"At your service, ma'am," he told her.

"When we leave here you leave with me." She leaned back in his arms, gazing up at him. "Okay?"

He nodded. "What is it?"

"Someone's trying to blackmail me."

He twirled her, let her go, and she came gliding back to him, grinding and bumping rhythmically, everything moving to the beat. Well now, he told himself, things are really adding up.

He was dancing with the blonde to slow music; they were dancing close and the scent of her, the feel of her and the memory of that afternoon were all combining to produce an extremely tonic effect on him. She was charging him up like a battery, lighting lights, flipping switches and ringing bells throughout his system, when O'Dell's man, Arturo, came out onto the terrace, bowed deeply to Mendoza and, with many *con permissos* and *por favors*, spoke to him, then Mendoza stopped dancing and clapped his hands and the music came to a rattling, plunking, clanking end and in the silence Johnny realized that there was no longer the monotonous overtone of the drill.

The expert was ready to open the safe, Mendoza announced, and he suggested that they all go and witness the event.

"That won't be necessary," Ross told him. "This is *business*, Alonzo. Irene and I are tired. We'll check the safe, then go to our rooms and get some sleep."

"I say there should be witnesses present," Mendoza declared tartly.

"Damn it, man, I'm the executor of Kim's estate!" Ross exclaimed.

"I still say there should be witnesses!" cried Mendoza. "Come everybody—on to O'Dell's!"

They all streamed out into the rear court and stepped through the door to O'Dell's upper terrace. Two men were leaning against the outside wall of O'Dell's bedroom and one of them held a thin steel rod which protruded from the back of the safe. They went into O'Dell's bedroom and Jervis Ross strode to the safe door and grasped the knob.

"*Listo!*" Arturo called sharply to the man with the rod.

There was a clanking noise then inside the safe as the tip of the rod tripped the locking mechanism and when Jervis Ross pulled on the knob the door of the safe swung open.

There was a sense of disappointment, at least among the three lovely ladies—Johnny could feel it. He guessed they had expected piles of emeralds, bars of gold and stacks of currency. As it was, there didn't appear to be much of anything inside the safe.

Mendoza clapped his hands and Arturo came running over to him. Mendoza whispered something and the man went hurrying off.

Jervis Ross took a Manila envelope out of the safe, examined the papers in it and put it back. He opened the two small drawers in the lower compartment and shut them and he peered into some steel boxes, and that, apparently, was it. When he turned from the safe he looked pale and tired. "It won't take long to inventory that," he remarked slowly, gazing at Mendoza.

MURDER ON HER MIND

"Jervis, old boy," Mendoza told him, "I really didn't bring everyone over here just to watch you open the safe. Oh no—I have another reason!"

Irene pointed. "What was in that big envelope?" she asked Ross.

"Insurance policies," Ross said. "Personal property policies on his stuff down here, policies on this house." He turned and stared into the safe again.

Outside, the man finished pounding lead into the hole he had made in the safe and Johnny could hear the other one mixing mortar to replace the bricks that had been knocked out. Then Oscar Wilde came streaking into the room with a wail, as if to say, "What's going on in here? What have I been missing?" The cat stalked over to Johnny and rubbed against his leg, and the eyes now were pale twin spotlights.

Arturo came hastening back with a silver bucket of ice and a magnum of champagne. He placed the bucket on the table behind the nearest couch and started twirling the bottle in the ice. A maid followed with a tray of glasses, and everyone's eyes were now on Mendoza. Catlike and wary, blonde, brunette and redhead moved to the couches, curled there, sleek, sinuous creatures with red claws. The champagne cork popped and Oscar Wilde leaped straight up and shot beneath the bed.

"Irene—" said Mendoza, gazing at that lady with burning eyes, "I hope you don't mind my having chosen this moment to make our announcement. I just decided that I simply can't wait. I'm so infernally *happy*—I want everyone to know!"

Once more a silence fell and in it the maid moved, serving the champagne. Arturo dropped an ice cube in an empty glass and handed it to Mendoza.

Mendoza raised the glass high. "I want you to know, dear friends," he declared, "that Irene has consented to become my wife, to live once more in this house—this time with me. Ladies and gentlemen, I give you my bride to be!" He touched the ice cube delicately to his lips.

"What a surprise!" the ladies on the couches caroled. "Oh, Alonzo, how perfectly splendid!" They rose, lifted their glasses. "To all happiness!" they said and, like three thirsty blossoms, sipped their bubbly.

Why pick that one, Johnny wondered—what with all this other nice stuff handy? He took a swallow of the champagne; then Mendoza, as if he had heard him thinking, answered him.

"You know why I love her?" Mendoza's eyes rested fondly upon the once-again bride to be. "Because she's the most utterly ruthless woman I ever met," Mendoza declared. "She has always completely fascinated me!"

Well, thought Johnny, it figures. He drained his glass and caught the black-haired lady's eye. Now let us blow, his glance suggested, you and me. And, though the lady nodded, it turned out they weren't going to get the chance quite yet to slip away; for, after everyone had congratulated Irene and taken leave of her and Ross, it was Mendoza who seized Rowena King and went skipping back to his house with her, while the blonde and the redhead twined themselves like seaweed around Johnny.

It was the hardest thing he had worked on, for the very simple reason that it was so hard to work; or—to put it another way—because the work got so mixed up with the pleasure. And, also, he would remember that there was always a Banker waiting—somewhere, sometime—to collect his overdraft on life. You got only one pass, and with loaded dice. Dead was dead, and maybe the cook's son did it. "Let's go for a swim!" they said. And who was he to spoil their fun?

Mendoza provided gaily colored cotton kerchiefs and in a trice the ladies vanished and reappeared, skimpily and haphazardly covered above and below, and then, like three loving sisters, full of O'Dell's vintages and bubbly, they began to frolic in the pool, pausing either to retrieve or adjust their attire now and then. It was a sight not to be missed, and Johnny missed none of it. He sat there sipping the Napoleon and puffing on one of the Havanas, while Mendoza capered up and down and around the pool, joining in the fun. Then the phone began to ring in Mendoza's bedroom and since, with all the gaiety, no one else appeared to hear the sound, he went in and answered.

"*Bueno,*" he said.

"I want to speak to Mrs. King," a man's voice told him.

He went out to the pool and got the black-haired lady, brought her into the bedroom. He watched her face as she said, "Hello," and as she listened, he saw by the look on her face that he should stay there.

"It's *him,*" she whispered, placing a hand over the mouthpiece. "The one who—"

"Tell him you'll meet him," he interrupted. He looked at his watch. "Tell him to be at your house in half an hour."

Rowena King repeated it into the mouthpiece, then she listened, shook her head. "He wants to know if I got the money."

"Tell him you want to see the evidence first. Then you'll get it."

She spoke once more, listened, cupped her hand over the mouthpiece. "He won't meet me unless I've got the money. I either have it by morning or else."

"Tell him you've got the money. Tell him to come to your house. You'll be waiting there. Tell him you want to hand the money to him personally and get what he's got."

She said it and when she hung up she stared at him. "How do you happen to know so much about it?"

"It's my business," he said. He picked up the phone. "Now get dressed. And hurry."

He got the operator and after a moment—probably partly because of the prestige of phoning from Mendoza's—she was able to tell him that the call had come from a pay booth in the hotel on the plaza. Then he phoned for a cab from the corner stand and as he put down the phone Rowena King, sheathed in velvet once more, came from the dressing room toweling her hair.

"Is there another way out of here?" he asked her.

She pointed to the archway, at the far side of the room. "That will take you out to the front court."

"Tell them I had a call and left," he said. "Tell them your little boy's sick or something and you've got to go. I'll meet you right away out front."

The way he had things figured, he realized now that it would be a mistake to have the others see him leave with Rowena.

The taxi was waiting when he went out and it was the Umpire who was driving, Bad Ball Manuel himself, back on the job again, and when Johnny opened the car door the inside smelled like mescal. He stood there waiting by the open car door and in a few minutes the black-haired lady slipped out of the house, her shawl over her head. He helped her in, then jumped in himself and they were off, jouncing and bouncing along over the broken, cobbled street toward the plaza.

"When did this thing start?" he asked her.

"Sunday morning," the lady said. "A woman phoned me from Mexico City. She said she had a very interesting photograph of O'Dell and me and if I didn't pay her twenty thousand dollars she was going to give the photograph to this man—the one I'm supposed to marry. He's due in here from Paris the last of the week."

"She had a picture of you in O'Dell's bed," he suggested. "Taken Saturday night."

"Nobody ever took a picture of me in O'Dell's bed," she said.

They passed a street light and for a brief, flickering moment he stared into her face. "You're sure?"

"Positive."

"But you did go back to O'Dell's Saturday night?"

"I'm not denying that, but nobody took my picture there," she said.

"You didn't fall asleep or something?"

"*Sleep?*" The idea seemed to amuse her. "No," she said. "I was only there about twenty minutes. Then my mother phoned in a big uproar—the guy was on the wire from Paris. Where the hell was I, he wanted to know. Why wasn't I home crocheting doilies or something, while I waited around for him. Jealous, you know. So I went home to return the call."

"You didn't go back to O'Dell's again afterward?"

"No," she said. "Kim wasn't much fun Saturday night."

"You said a woman phoned you first. When did the man get into the act?"

"He phoned this afternoon. 'I know you can get it, so get it up,' he said. 'I'm not fooling you, beautiful. I hate to do this to anybody, let alone a real doll like you, but you've got it and I haven't. And I'm the one that right now needs it. Bad, honey. So, if you don't get it up right now, something unpleasant is going to happen. To you, doll.' He said that, then he stopped. 'Or maybe to your little boy Jeffrey,' he said."

"What did you say to that?"

"I dropped that phone," she said. "Then I called a car and sent my mother and the nursemaid up to Mexico City with Jeffrey."

"Did the man's voice sound familiar?"

She said, "I think he was disguising it. The woman was disguising hers, I know. Anyhow, I didn't recognize his voice. I thought he sounded interesting till I realized what he was saying to me."

They had come upon the plaza now, the car emerging from the quiet side street into the carnival blare. The carnival was still going strong, with whirling lights, jangling melodies, the crackle of the target rifles and the cries of pitchmen; then the speaker began once more, a gargantuan night voice wailing of love.

He left the lady to wait in the cab and entered the hotel. There were three telephone booths across the lobby from the registration desk, but the desk clerk could only shrug and smile apologetically when he asked him if he had noticed anyone using them lately. He located a bellboy and got the same response.

So that was that; he really hadn't expected more. He went back out to the cab and the Umpire drove them over the tortuous route to Rowena's house.

From the first, from the moment that Oscar Wilde had presented him with that flashbulb, he had figured the lack-haired lady as the subject of some illicit photography. Mendoza had told him she had money and planned to marry more. Also, the blackmail pattern was always a triangular one, a nasty trinity. Number one was the picture taker, number two was one of the two people in the picture, and number three was the person that number two wouldn't want to see the picture.

It had figured; it still did. Even the fact that the lady vowed there had been no picture taken fitted. He had a possible explanation now for that unused flashbulb and he felt sure that the man who had phoned—the desperate one, who knew all about the lady, knew she had money and told her to get it up, or else— was the one who had killed O'Dell.

CHAPTER TWELVE

ROWENA UNLOCKED the little door in the tall blue gates and they walked up the drive toward the house. Through the open living room they could see the moon repeat itself in the pool and the air was warm and sexy, heavy with the sweet, cloying fragrance of *huele de noche*, that lovers' shrub that gives off its scent only in the night, and now they could hear again that great night voice in the distant plaza whispering of love.

The lady touched his arm, stopped him, and he looked down into her lovely moon-drenched face. "I'm in danger maybe, aren't I?" she whispered.

He nodded. "Could be."

"You won't leave me, will you?"

"Not for a while," he said. "You're going to be my bait."

"That's a term of endearment, maybe?" She moved in against him.

"I mean I hope that guy takes a big, crazy chance and comes here," he said.

He breathed deeply, looked away from her, and now he saw the snowy peak of Popo thrusting up like a mirage below the moon and now that night fragrance had seeped into his blood. Her arms crept around him beneath his coat, the great night voice whispered more urgently and her velvet pressure had become insistent. He pulled her to him then and met the ripe, scarlet splendor of her lips.

❈   ❈   ❈

Where had the night gone? Had the bell on the gate rung?

Now the air hung more heavily, lay like a fragrant, humid blanket on their skins, and through the windows he could see a strange purplish light that could be a promise of dawn. Then some macabre bird suddenly sang down the scale in the jacaranda tree outside the windows and at the same instant his eyes fell upon the traveling clock that stood on the table beside the bed.

Nine-fifteen, the hands on the clock said, and as he stared in disbelief at that news there was a huge bass muttering sound to the north, a Jovian rumbling, and he sprang up then and went to the windows to see that it was indeed morning, with great purple cloud masses, all boiling and tossing and rushing south, completely obscuring the sky.

The muttering sounds grew swiftly louder and there was a sudden burst of wind that set the palm fronds clacking; then another gust of wind swept through the windows, damp and cool, and now, as the wind rose in strength and purpose, he could hear servants shouting and running. He could hear them securing the flapping shutters, drawing the canvas draperies that protected the open living room. An instant later the jacaranda tree leaped forth whitely from the purple shadow, as in a camera flash, and the tremendous crash that followed brought Rowena flying from the bed into his arms.

As the high wind continued he comforted her and when the thunder rolled on south and the rain came pouring down he waited it out with her, pleasantly enough. After all, he thought, he couldn't go anywhere in that deluge, and he really didn't feel that old Mrs. O'Dell, up there in San Francisco, would expect him to.

In about half an hour, when the clouds ran out of rain, he phoned for a cab, and once more, as he dressed, that Cassandra of a bird sang ominously down scale.

"So he didn't come," the lady said, watching him strap on his gun.

He shook his head. "Don't let anybody in. Meanwhile, I'll go find him."

"How are you going to find him when you don't know who he is?"

"I think I know somebody who does know," he said.

He was ready to leave and for a moment he gazed at her, a satisfied, satin-tan Lorelei on a white satin sheet. "*Adios*," he told her then.

"I'll see you tonight?"

"*Lady*—" he said slowly.

She smiled a lazy little smile, looking up at him through half-lowered lashes. "Tomorrow?"

"Tomorrow?" He moved to the door, turned there and tried to shrug off the somber feeling he had. "Who knows?" he told her. "Approximately like the man said: Tomorrow I myself could be with yesterday's seven thousand years.'"

Go with God, then," she whispered.

And, as she said it, thunder rumbled once more to the north; and, in the words of Omar, he had spoken more truly than he knew.

The sky was boiling again as he got into the cab. Purple clouds were rushing down, hurling their great bolts, rocking the town with thunder, and all the way to the plaza the taxi was swept along by a following surf of wind-driven rain.

The plaza was desolate in the rain. The amusement booths were shuttered and there were people huddled beneath the old trees. The canvas top of the merry-go-round was bellying and flapping and the seats of the Ferris wheel were swaying wildly, creaking and groaning, while the skeleton of the wheel itself loomed weirdly above the treetops, a spectral relic of amusement against the ferocious sky.

Their thunder was like their music, he thought—real loud. The hotel lobby sounded like the inside of a drum during the final movement of a big Wagnerian number, and, when he had braved the peril of the outside stair to his room, he could hear the slats of the blinds chattering, feel the stinging rain at his back and see the walls of the rooms shudder.

He had been going to shave and have some breakfast before he went to visit the blonde; but, as it was, he did neither, for there was a note for him. The note, written in pencil on a sheet of hotel stationery, lay on his bureau, held down by a water glass.

Translated, the message read: "I found an extra face towel in the bath of the American mister who stays in room 218." It was signed "Your maid of the afternoon."

He went out and down along the balcony to 218. The windows were shut, the blinds closed. There was only the frenzied sound of the storm. After a moment he turned the knob, the door opened a crack and, through it, the room gulped air. He drew his gun then and slipped inside, almost firing at the flurry of cards that whirled up from the table in the center of the room.

The table had been covered with the spread from one of the twin beds and was littered with poker chips and playing cards. There were ashtrays filled with butts, and on the bureau were bottles and glasses and coffee cups and the room smelled dankly of cigarette and cigar smoke; then he recognized the other odor there—the caustic scent of burned gunpowder. At the same moment he saw the shoe, a shoe with a foot in it, protruding from behind the farther bed.

Lightning made the blinds glow brightly for an instant and, in the vacuum that followed, bedspreads and cards stirred, then the crash came, slapped the hotel, bounced off and rumbled away, spilling its echoes through the town. And after that there was just the wind again, fierce gusts whistling along the balcony, trying to unfasten the windows, flinging pellets of rain against them. In this moment of comparative silence he bolted the door and moved on into the room.

The man was lying on his back beside the bed. He was a tall man, fully dressed, no longer young; yet, even in death, he looked good. He appeared to take his new status quite casually, Johnny thought. Then he recognized the face, was able—perhaps because it was an unusual one—to recall the man's name. The name was Gallatin. He was the man who had come up and spoken to the two gentlemen from the great Southwest at lunch the day before and had been introduced to their women-folk.

Now there was blood on Mr. Gallatin's shirt front, right above the heart. The blood still glistened wetly and, when Johnny knelt and took the gun the man had not quite succeeded in drawing from the waistband of his pants the hand that held the gun was still warm and limp. And, if it wasn't the gun he had taken from the red-haired lady, he thought, then it was certainly its twin, even to the five bright, unfired cartridges it contained.

He had slipped his own gun back into its holster and was still kneeling there with the .32 while he pondered for a moment, when all of a sudden the various elements of the situation added up with such a bang that he was scarcely aware of the thunderclap that immediately followed his addition.

Once more the thunder went rolling south toward the mountains of Guerrero; then in the demi-stillness of the aftermath, things stirred and twitched and for a moment the walls appeared to be breathing. And now hair that wasn't there tried to rise and the perpendicular chill spread from his spine, ran out like cold fingers along lateral nerves.

From where he knelt he could see the top of the bathroom door reflected in the mirror above the bureau. The door was open a few inches and it had stirred. As he watched it in the mirror the door moved again, but it was not the kind of eerie, minor movement that he had come to expect from the drafts that sucked at the room. There was a will behind the movement of the door, and the will decreed that the door should move steadily inward, by fractions of inches be opened wider.

He knew now that tiny, out-of-phase movement of the door must have registered itself upon his senses, if not his consciousness, moments before and only when things suddenly added up had it come to have imperative meaning, instantly become part of the blood not yet dry, the warm limpness of that hand, and of another odor besides smoke—shaving lotion. The scent of the lotion was keen and fresh there by the body, and it did not emanate from Mr. Gallatin, for he wore a night's growth of beard.

Things had added; then, before he had consciously looked at the door or had time to reason, his senses, in independent wisdom, had alerted him. And all this—the addition, the alerting and even the review thereof—occurred only in the instant it took him to focus his eyes on the mirror and really observe the movement of the door.

Before the next instant could pass he had swung and fired the .32, turning to one side as he did so, diving and firing twice again through the door as he bounced on the tiles, and at some point during this activity it felt as if he had been slapped on the neck with a hot curling iron.

The explosions, coming so close together as to be almost simultaneous and mingling with the thunder had a numbing effect on his hearing and still as all the echoes died he could hear the toilet gurgle once more and he was also aware of a faint, slow sliding sound, then the bathroom door moved from inward to outward, slammed shut, and there was a clatter of steel on tile.

He put a hand to his neck and it still felt hot from the touch of the lead, but the skin had scarcely been broken. There was almost no blood.

When he opened the bathroom door he had to put his weight against the door in order to push the body aside, then he snapped on the light and stood gazing down at the Banker. The Banker lay there on the florid tile in his dark silk suit and all three shots had hit him, one of them in the head.

He didn't touch the gun on the floor but he did pick up the pigskin wallet that lay beside the gun. There were several hundred dollars in the wallet and a State of Nevada driver's license issued two months before in the name of George C. Gallatin, who gave a permanent address in New York City. There was also a folded telegram.

The telegram came from Las Vegas. It was dated the previous Wednesday and addressed to Gallatin at that hotel.

PAY UP, the message read. WE MEAN IT. And that was all. There was no signature.

He returned the telegram to the wallet, snapped off the bathroom light and went back into the bedroom. He put the wallet in the inside pocket of Gallatin's coat, where it belonged, and he wiped off the .32 and placed it in Gallatin's right hand. Then he looked in the closet. He opened the drawers of the bureau, and in the bottom drawer, among some dirty shirts, he found a camera. It was a popular, inexpensive make, sold in drugstores everywhere. Beside the camera there was a flash attachment, with a used bulb still in the socket, and there was a package of bulbs with two of the bulbs missing. The bulbs were Number 5, the same size as the one in his pocket.

The noisy second front of the storm had moved on south when he stepped out onto the balcony and the rain was coming straight down. As he entered his room and turned to shut the door he saw two maids coming up the stairs, followed by a waiter with a breakfast tray.

As for himself, the sights in room 218 had robbed him of any appetite for breakfast, nor was he in the mood to shave. He did apply a styptic pencil to the bullet crease on his neck, however, and he changed his shirt. As he was buttoning the clean shirt he heard a scream somewhere, then one of the maids came running back past his windows and he heard her go pattering down the stairs.

By the time he got a cab and was headed along past the plaza toward the blonde's he could already hear a siren wailing, coming from the direction of the police station and going toward the hotel.

CHAPTER THIRTEEN

THERE WAS no one behind the desk in Helen's hotel and Johnny went on up the stairs and down the tiled hall to her room. He tried the door but it was locked and so he knocked on it, waited, then knocked again.

"Who is it?" the lady called, and he could tell by the sound of her voice that she had been asleep.

"It's George," he said.

After a moment he heard a bolt slide and when he opened the door she was on her way back to the bed. She got to the bed and sat down on it before she looked at him, then her eyes widened.

"What's the George game?" she asked him.

"George C. Gallatin," he said. "I've been talking to him."

"Oh?" she crawled under the sheet, propped herself up on one elbow and gazed at him. "What did George have to say?"

"Well," he said, "it was kind of a one-way conversation." He went over and sat down in the chair by the bed. "George is dead," he told her.

"Go on," she said.

"George is dead."

She sat up. "*No*—" she whispered.

He nodded. "Hits you pretty hard, does it?"

"I don't believe you," she said. "How do you know?"

He told her then about losing the gun he had taken from Eleanor and how he had found the gun again, only the way he told it the man in the bathroom was dead when he went in there; and, while he was speaking, two big tears appeared in her eyes, popped out and slid slowly down her cheeks; then, when he was finished, she lay back on the pillow and stared hard at the ceiling.

'What made you connect George and me?" she asked him finally.

"Well," he said, "maybe we better start from the beginning. I would guess you met George in Las Vegas while you were there getting your divorce."

She nodded. "He was fun," she said. "Till just lately when he got so nervous, George was loads of fun."

"After he got that telegram he got nervous?"

"Yes," she said.

"I would also guess he lost some money up there in Las Vegas."

"He lost what I got from J. Stuart Wellington," she said. "Then he signed some I.O.U's."

"About twenty thousand dollars' worth?" he suggested.

"How did you know that?" she asked. She propped herself up again and took a cigarette from a package of Mexican ones on the bedside table.

"George told another lady that he was badly in need of that amount," he said. He lit the cigarette for her, met her eyes.

"I still don't get it," she declared. "How did you connect George and me?"

"A number of things added up in your favor," he told her. "One was that you were in Las Vegas. But that was just a kind of clincher. I didn't begin with that. Another thing—that gun was taken from my room while I was here with you yesterday. It's my guess you had the clerk tell me to wait a while before I came up so that you could phone George and tell him about the gun. You knew I had it. Mendoza had passed on that item."

"Other people knew you had that gun too," she said. "How about that redhead with the slushy southern accent you took it from?"

"Just be patient," he told her. "Remember—you admitted you went to that hotel Saturday night after you left O'Dell's." He gazed at her. "And yesterday morning you got out of a taxi that had brought you down from Mexico City and went in there again."

"How do you know I was in Mexico City?"

"One thing—you were dressed for the city. Another—I took that same cab to Mendoza's. It was a nice day here, but the driver said he hit rain in the mountains on the way down from the city."

"So what?"

"So what say we stop beating the bushes?" he told her. "You were in a blackmail setup with this George character. You called Rowena King from Mexico City. My guess is that you went up there to get the picture you took Saturday night developed."

Helen blew out smoke. "I don't know what you're talking about."

"If that's the way it is," he said, "then I'm going to have to turn the information I have over to the police."

"What information?"

He stood up. "I think," he said, "that you either shot O'Dell yourself or were an accessory to his murder."

He turned and started for the door, but he didn't get there. She was on his back like a cat. "Get off," he told her.

"Be nice!"

He returned to the bed, unfastened her grip on his neck and dumped her. "Well?" he said, gazing down at her.

"You haven't got anything on me," she told him. "If you go to the police I'll just have to tell them you tried to rape me and you're mad because I wouldn't let you."

"What did George do with his own gun?"

VECHEL HOWARD

"George didn't have a gun," she said. "That's why he took that one from you."

He sat down. "Now wait," he told her. He studied her face. "Don't you want to tell me the truth?"

"I asked you to be nice," she said. "If you're nice I'll tell you things. Men are always getting serious, then they get nervous and they aren't fun."

"Okay," he said. "I'm nice. Tell me things."

She shook her head. "I can't talk, not with you just sitting there with all your clothes on staring at me in that cold, pitiless way. You make me feel so guilty. And I'm not guilty, not of anything except trying to help somebody in trouble."

"What do you want me to do," he asked her, "go over in a corner and stand on my head?"

"No," she said. "I feel so lonely and miserable and I've had a big shock and I'm kind of scared." She gazed at him. "I want somebody to hold me."

"No," he said.

"Okay," she whispered. "Then you'll never find out!" She waited a moment. "I *want* to tell you," she said, "because I don't want you believing I could be guilty of something bad."

What would old Mrs. O'Dell have him do? he wondered wearily. He stood up then and took off his coat.

It was a good-while later before the blonde-haired lady got into the mood for talking. She lay snuggled cosily against him, tracing pictures on his chest while the rain poured down outside and presently she spoke. "It's funny," she remarked in a thoughtful way.

"What is?" he asked her.

"How things work out," she said. "I start with old J. Stuart Wellington and end up with you. If it hadn't been for J. Stuart I wouldn't have gone to Las Vegas and met George, or that ex-wife of Kim O'Dell's. And if somebody hadn't killed O'Dell I wouldn't be here with you right now."

"Some rainy Tuesday," he suggested, 'let's get together and figure out who killed O'Dell."

"It's Tuesday," she said. "And it's raining. I'm pretty smart, you know. I think you mean today. You mean right now—don't you?"

"Yes," he said. "Those boys in Las Vegas play for keeps. George Gallatin was in bad trouble, so you tried to help him out. There wasn't any angle you could blackmail O'Dell on, but that King doll was vulnerable."

"Oh, it wasn't *her* money George was after," she said. "It was this jerk's, this Charlie Scourby's, the man she's going to marry. Did you ever hear of him?"

"He's the one in Paris?"

"Sure. He comes from Oklahoma and he makes oil-drilling tools or something. He's over there on some big international deal. George knew all about him. Charlie Scourby's worth fifty million dollars, George said; and, what's more, he's one of the biggest, meanest bastards that ever lived—but crazy about that King gal. That guy wouldn't even miss twenty grand, George said. All King would have to do was phone him, tell him she was in a jam and needed the money and that Charlie Scourby would just send a cable and then somebody would be at King's house in half an hour with the cash."

"How did you know King was going to be with O'Dell Saturday night?"

"Well," she said, "I knew I wasn't. And he and the redhead had a big fuss. Anyhow, I knew it was King's turn."

"What time did you and George go there?"

"About three A.M.," she said.

"Why so late?"

Slightly embarrassed, she cleared her throat. "You see there was a little ritual to those things. First you would sit around and drink a little brandy and play some music. And then—well, you know how it is. And then there would be a bubble bath together maybe. And then—well, you know how it is some more."

"So you timed it?"

"Sure," she said. "Why not?"

"What happened?" he asked softly.

"Well—" She began another picture on his chest. "Nothing really. I let us into the back court of Mendoza's with my little key, then into Kim's. We went along like mice to his bedroom door and George stood there with the camera, but he couldn't see anything and he couldn't hear anything."

"So he tossed a flashbulb in," he said. "Then he snapped a picture and O'Dell came lunging for him. You said the guy was nervous, didn't you?"

"Yes," she said. "George was nervous."

"So he pulled the trigger."

"Huh-*uh*," she said. "Listen—he threw a flashbulb in, then he heard a movement on the bed and he snapped the picture. Then we got out of there fast."

"What did George see when the flashbulb went off?"

"He didn't. He blinked."

"So you got a picture of O'Dell alone. That right?"

"Yes, he was alone."

He shook his head slowly. "I won't buy it," he told her. "Look— you don't need to protect that George character now. He's dead. And I'm not the law. I'm not going to do anything to you. I just want to be able to go back there to San Francisco and tell O'Dell's mother what happened."

"I told you what happened."

"All except the one big thing—that after George Gallatin took the picture he shot O'Dell; then he got rid of that hot gun."

She sat up. "Gee," she said sadly, "you really trust me, don't you?"

"The ladies I *never* trust," he said. Then he watched her swing from the bed, saw her cross the tiles on tiptoe to the bureau and start rummaging through a drawer.

"You went up to Mexico City to get the picture developed," he said. "You still thought you had gotten a picture of her in that bed with him."

"We thought so," she agreed. She was looking through a purse.

"You called her before you got the picture developed."

"That's right," she said, and now she had found what she was looking for—an envelope. She returned to the bed and handed it to him.

"What is it?" he asked.

"The picture," she said.

In the envelope there was a negative and one print of a photograph. The photograph was of O'Dell and, sure enough, he was alone. He was lying on the floor of his bedroom in his birthday suit, a hole in his head, while Oscar Wilde looked straight into the camera from the bed.

CHAPTER FOURTEEN

THE RAIN HAD STOPPED by the time he got out of there. The sky was blue once more and the midday sun beat down with a baleful intensity. The water was running off, choking the gutters, and everything was steaming, even the wet people.

As he walked back through the plaza they were taking the shutters off the carnival booths and a couple of men were trying to start the old engine that ran the merry-go-round; then suddenly the big voice of the speaker screeched and boomed, flooding the town with music again, startling the birds out of the trees and sending them off in wild, swooping flight.

There was a crowd in front of the hotel that was breaking up and the street was filled with little groups discussing the shooting and so was the hotel lobby. He went through the lobby to the garden and when he looked up along the balcony he saw a maid with a mop and bucket going into 218. The police had come and gone, he thought, and now business would be good at *Quo Vadis*.

Eleanor called "Come in" when he knocked and when he opened the door she was lying on the bed in that tricky striped silk robe of hers, her red hair spread over the pillows.

"You look all burnt out, honey," she declared. "What have you been doing? I phoned you and phoned you. Where've you been?"

He moved toward her. "Did you have something to tell me?"

She said, "If you're going to keep me hanging around here I just do think you ought to pay some attention to me."

He nodded. "I'm going to," he said. "How about a drink?"

"That's *one* good idea," she said. She moved, stretched her long amber legs and gave him a deep, warm look. "Got more?"

"Yes, I have." He picked up the phone and ordered the drinks, then he gazed at her and said, "He was what you'd call a real cad down your way, wasn't he, ma'am? I expect if some of your men kin had been around they would have horsewhipped him for what he did to you."

Her eyes had widened. "Honey," she said slowly, "what have you been smoking?"

"I'm talking about O'Dell," he told her. "And you. O'Dell led you to believe he planned to marry you, didn't he?"

"I told you he made noises that sounded that way."

"You took him seriously, anyhow."

"Yes, I did."

"Then suddenly it was all off. He was going on a trip, didn't know when he was coming back, and you were left holding the bag."

For a moment her eyes blazed. "Maybe he deserved what he got. Don't you think?"

"Most juries would let you off," he agreed. "He hit you too, didn't he?"

"No," she said. She looked suddenly startled. She frowned at him. "Honey, what are you talking about?"

"My other bright idea for the day is that you killed O'Dell," he said.

"Well, you just better get rid of that one," she advised him.

He got up and paced to the windows, then came back. "It happens to be an idea I may be able to prove."

"I told you exactly what I did Saturday night," she said.

"Maybe you don't remember," he suggested. "Maybe your desire not to remember was so powerful that you simply blacked out the memory."

"What memory, honey?"

"Getting drunk, calling a taxi, going and shooting O'Dell."

"No," she said. "I sure don't remember anything like that."

The boy came with their drinks then and he paid him, tipped him and he took her drink to her. *"Vivas,"* she said, lifting her glass.

"Look—" he told her, "I want to give you a break. I don't want to hand you over to the local police and have you tossed into some dirt-floored jail with scorpions and low, unwashed characters, maybe let you rot in there a year or two before they get around to trying you.

"Good Lord!" she exclaimed. "Stop *talkin'* like that."

"Just tell me the truth," he said. "Tell me how it happened; then we'll go up to Mexico City and you can surrender yourself to our embassy there. They'll see that you get the best legal counsel, and that all your rights as an American citizen are protected. As I said, most juries would let you off in the States, and the same will be true here."

"Honey," she declared, "I think you need a little sleep."

He sat down and picked up the phone. "Well," he said, "I had to try it on you for size, ma'am. Now maybe we can find out how good it fits."

He asked the operator to get him the police station and he told the man who answered that he wished to speak to Chief Guiterrez. The chief was apparently eating a snack; he was chewing when he answered and his voice sounded as if he had just found tacks in his tortillas.

"I heard about the shooting here at the hotel," Johnny told him after he had identified himself.

"Why do they want to come down here to kill each other?" the chief complained bitterly. "Why can't they stay home and do it?"

"I was just wondering," Johnny told him, "if you saw any connection between the affair this morning and the O'Dell case."

"*Señor!*" the chief exclaimed. "What possible connection could there be? I told you—we are looking for the man who we believe most certainly killed *Señor* O'Dell. The son of the cook, *señor.*"

"I was wondering about the guns used this morning—" Johnny said. "I thought perhaps one of the guns might have been of the same caliber as the gun that fired the bullet you found in Q'Dell's bedroom."

"There was a gun of that caliber used this morning," the chief agreed. "We are not entirely *estupido* here, señor. The police *laboratorio* in Mexico City has identified the bullet that killed Señor O'Dell as one that was fired from a certain make of gun. The gun of the same .32 caliber used by one of the Americanos this morning, señor, was of a different make."

Johnny put down the phone and gazed at the red-haired lady. "Okay," he said wearily. "You can take it off. It won't fit you."

He got up again and paced while she lay on the bed and watched him. "Now, boy, you're right back where you began," he told himself aloud. "It was that flash-bulb threw you off. It kept your nose glued to a trail that led you right back to where you started."

"What flashbulb, honey?"

"Never mind," he said. "Anyhow, that bulb suggested a pattern, and I was right, only I was wrong. Meanwhile, what didn't fit the pattern I ignored."

"Why don't you relax," she suggested, "and quit ignoring the really pleasant things in life?"

"Now I've got to go back," he said. "I've got to pick up bits of things and try to paste them together into a picture." He went over and sat down on the edge of the bed. "Tell me what you know about Irene Maybrick."

"Well," she said, 'she was Kim's last wife. She got a divorce a couple of years ago and custody of the little boy she and Kim had, who now inherits all Kim's money. As I understand it, this fellow Maybrick, a real lady killer and kind of a ne'er-do-well fellow, came down here and Irene fell for him. She got the divorce to marry him; then Irene, I hear, ran through all the money she got from Kim and took off with somebody else."

"What about her and Ross?"

"How do you mean, honey?"

"Anything romantic between them?"

"If there is or was I never heard tell of it," she said. "And it was no surprise to me last night when Alonzo made the big announcement that he was going to marry Irene. They were carrying on most hot and heavy together when she was down last month."

"Tell me this," he said. "Do you know why O'Dell was going up to San Francisco? I gather it was a sudden decision. His mother didn't say anything about it."

"As far as I know he only decided to go on Friday or maybe even Saturday," she said. "And I gathered it was business."

"I've heard he seemed upset Saturday night."

"Yes," she said. "I think it was business. I know this much—he wanted to buy into come uranium-mining company down here. I know because he entertained the man who owned the company at his house for dinner when I was there. Kim had Ross send him down some municipal bonds—some kind of bonds, anyhow, that weren't negotiable, you know, that he was going to put up for security. Irene brought the bonds down when she came last month. She went to a hotel there in Mexico City after she got off the plane and somebody stole the bonds, so Kim had to make this man with the mining company wait until new bonds could be issued, or maybe he was going to get some other securities or sell something. I don't know, but I think that's why he suddenly decided to go to San Francisco and I think that's why he was upset."

He rose abruptly. "Thanks," he said. "I'd have been further along with this thing maybe if I'd just sat around yakking with you instead of knocking myself out chasing up and down this town."

"That's what I keep *tellin'* you, honey."

"I'll check with you later, ma'am."

There was a big, dazzling flash of amber and she came off the bed. "Is that a promise?"

"It is," he said, then he opened the door and got out.

CHAPTER FIFTEEN

W HILE HE WAITED for the operator to complete his call he sat on one of the beds, holding the phone and drawing circles on the cover of his notebook.

Put half a dozen people together, he thought, and it was like drawing the same number of circles, circles that touched or over-lapped one another in varying degree. Now he had followed the three likeliest circles around and gotten nowhere except dizzy and on this next set, he thought, he wasn't only starting back where he had begun when he first went to talk to Mendoza—he was starting clear back in San Francisco.

After another minute he got the call through to his San Francisco office and he told his secretary, Bess, to phone old Mrs. O'Dell and find out if Jervis Ross had her son's power of attorney, had been able to sign for O'Dell, buy and sell for him. Then he told Bess the kind of a check he wanted made on Ross and Irene. He told her to put several men on it because he would like her to phone him back with what she had by five o'clock.

When he finished talking to Bess he ordered a *filete*, some fried beans and a couple of bottles of dark beer and by the time he had shaved and showered the food was there. He ate slowly and drank the beer, then he lay down on one of the beds and promptly fell asleep.

And, almost at once, it seemed, into his dream and through the muffled, jangling, many-throated blare of the carnival, a small insistent bell penetrated and he opened his eyes, surprised to see the soft late-afternoon light seeping through the blinds, and it was still hot. He was sweating as he reached for the phone.

It was Bess's voice, coming from far away up there in the fog. "Here you are," said Bess. "Here's what I've got. Jervis Ross had Kim O'Dell's unlimited power of attorney. He had handled all O'Dell's investments for many years, made out his income tax, and so on. He's executor of the estate, and he and a junior partner are trustees for the boy, who inherits, and who is now in a private school at Pebble Beach."

The voice paused as there was a crackle on the line from some distant storm. "You hear me?"

"I hear you," he said.

"Ross's wife is divorcing him. She lives down in Hillsborough. Ross has an apartment here on Jackson Street, not far from Irene Maybrick's. They visit each other, frequently spend the night together. I'm still checking the airlines. Wouldn't Mrs. O'Dell have phoned Mrs. Maybrick Sunday morning and told her of Kim O'Dell's death?"

"No," he said. "The old lady wouldn't have anything to do with Irene. She was going to leave it to Ross to tell her."

"You want me to find out if she may have taken a plane down there Saturday instead of the one she's supposed to have taken with Ross on Sunday?"

"That's it," he said. "All I want you to do is check to see if she actually did get on a plane there Sunday; then call me back. If I'm not here tell the operator to ring me at O'Dell's."

He had not entered the slice of tropic paradise that had been O'Dell's from the street on which it fronted before, and it was a memorable experience to have the gates of the great court creak open, to have the porter bow you in as if you were some bejeweled rajah on an elephant, to look up and see those climbing tiers of terraces and gardens, the ascending levels of house that had been created by Alonzo Mendoza from the old convent.

Arturo in his striped vest was waiting for him on the terrace that flowed into the living room. Arturo bowed. "Good afternoon, Señor Church."

Johnny replied in kind, then said, "I wish to speak to Señor Ross and la Señora Maybrick, *por favor.*"

Arturo looked surprised. "But they have gone, señor," he said. "*Gone?*"

"They left right after lunch to take a plane back to the States." Johnny stared at him. "Are they coming back?" he asked.

"I understand that the señora will come back," Arturo said. "I understand that she will be the lady of the house here again when Señor Mendoza is once more *patrón.*"

He pondered a moment. Did he really need their presence, he wondered? Maybe so, maybe not. "In any case," he told Arturo, "I would like to make another small investigation in that bedroom."

"*Sí, señor!*"

Arturo turned and led him up the stairs and gently rising walks to the upper terrace. He opened the door of O'Dell's bedroom, stood aside as Johnny entered, then followed him in.

Johnny went directly over to the wall where the safe and the filecase were concealed by the paneling. He slid back the paneling, dialed the proper combination on the filecase lock and pulled out the upper drawer.

The drawer was partially filled with file folders. Most of the folders contained correspondence. There was a folder with letters to and from the government concerning the duty on an imported car, one containing communications with a charitable institution to which O'Dell appeared to have been a heavy contributor, letters connected with local taxes and insurance, household inventories, receipted bills.

The only folder that was empty was one marked *Ross*.

Johnny shut the drawer, slid back the paneling and turned, and as he did so Oscar Wilde leaped in from the balcony onto the bed, glared at him inquiringly and yowled. "Well!" he seemed to say. "When are you going to get the lard out, boy, and wrap this thing up?" "If a telephone call comes for me here," Johnny told Arturo, "I will be at Señor Mendoza's."

"*Sí, señor.*

"Can you let me through the door into the rear court of Señor Mendoza?"

"*Sí, señor.*"

He saw Angelita standing there as Arturo closed the door in the wall behind him. The big voice in the plaza was wailing and Angelita was leaning against the wall at the top of the dark stair that led beneath the house, her head tilted back, her eyes shut, singing softly.

When the door was closed her eyes opened, met his, and she colored and started down the stairs, but he went after her and caught her. "Little Angel," he said, holding her hand, "you sing as pretty as you are."

They stood now at the head of a large subterranean room, in which the vaulted ceiling, walls and floor were of smooth, wine-dark stone. Other stairs led up into the kitchen, where there were voices and someone was rattling pots. Against one wall there was a worktable on which lay two freshly killed pheasants while other wild fowl hung in a rack above the table. At the end of the room were the cubicles where the nuns had slept and in one of them, on a narrow iron bed covered with a spread of pink sateen, he saw the big white rabbit from the carnival booth that the girl had been carrying the day before. The rabbit sat leaning back against the head of the bed, one ear tilting forward rakishly.

"I just wanted to find out how that boy friend of yours is?" he said.

"I have none, señor!" She laughed, gazing down at the hand that held her own, then someone in the kitchen shouted her name and she flashed a look up at him. "Always calling me! Angelita! Angelita!"

"Little Angel," he told her, "I'll see you later." He bent and kissed a golden cheek.

Dusk was falling as he stepped out onto the terrace and Alonzo Mendoza had just put a record on the turn-table of the player in his living room. As he saw his guest Mendoza snapped off the record with a screech. "Anything, to drown out that beastly caterwauling!" he declared. 'That carnival-all that amplified moaning of love! That's something you've done to us, my friend, you people up there. You love moaners, you gadget makers, you cocktail guzzlers!" He laughed, as if in appreciation of his own explosive verve, then bounced forward to shake Johnny's hand. "I telephoned you!" he said. I thought you might care to dine with me—just the two of us, so we can talk."

"Thank you," Johnny told him. "That suits me fine."

They settled themselves in chairs by the pool and when Mendoza clapped his hands his man came hurrying to find out Johnny's desires and Johnny said to Mendoza that if it would not offend anyone too much he would like a rum on the rocks.

Now tell me, Mendoza went on, when the man left to get the drink, what progress are you making in your detection? The ladies tell me that you have been giving them a regular whirl, still I have the feeling they are not telling me everything any more, the way they did. They're all quite mad about you! What is it you *do* to them?"

Johnny picked up the glass the man set down on the table beside him and took a swallow. "*Well—*" he said slowly.

I suppose it's because you are *young!*" Mendoza interrupted. "Oh, yes, that always gets them—youth itself does. But just wait till you're older, dear fellow. Then it takes *finesse*, you know. Tactics, technique." He paused. "And then, of course, you do carry a gun—*don't* you?"

Johnny gazed at him. "Yes."

"Well, you see that lends an aura of excitement, of danger. Then, too, you are a *big* young man; they sense in you the possible brute, the dominant male factor—and they *want* to be dominated as well as caressed. And, also, you are the quiet type. Children that they are, they believe that must portend you are thinking— deep thoughts, perhaps, that they, in their helpless femininity, could not possibly hope to understand."

The man came with a tray containing nuts and set it on the table. Then for a moment, while Johnny lit a cigarette, Mendoza sat crunching the nuts with his big well-preserved teeth and sipping soda water. A star appeared in the pool, and it was still hot, and the air was humid from the rain.

Mendoza dabbed at his lips with a little napkin. "Well!" he cried. "Speak, dear fellow. Remember our rules—you don't have to tell me all. That is, not unless you *wish* to tell me all. At any rate, I'm most eager to know of anything you may have accomplished so far, any discoveries you have made, or conclusions you may have come to."

"Well," Johnny told him, "I have done some spade-work, sir. I have, in fact, dug trenches that maybe I didn't need to dig. And maybe I have wasted a little time, but I have familiarized myself pretty thoroughly with the situation. And right now I've got two possible conclusions rattling around in my head."

"You wouldn't hint to me your conclusions, would you?"

"When I narrow the two down to one certain one I will tell you what it is."

"And when do you think you may do that?" Mendoza asked.

"Tonight," Johnny said.

"Well, fancy!" Mendoza exclaimed. He gazed at him with great interest. "Do either of your conclusions match the one held by the police?"

He shook his head. "I'm afraid not."

"They're just stupid fools, then?"

"I didn't say that."

Mendoza chuckled, then he thoughtfully crunched a few more nuts, Meanwhile, the servants had begun to lay the table for dinner and more stars had appeared in the pool, and now the distant medley of sounds that was the carnival had risen in pitch.

"Tell me," said Mendoza, "how do you make your deductions, arrive at your conclusions? Do you have textbooks, a lexicon, perhaps, a syllabus of criminology to which you refer?"

"I fly by the seat of my pants," Johnny told him. "I ask questions, I observe. I paste together bits of things to make pictures, and when I have a picture that seems to fit the situation I test it—I see if I can make it prove out. Do you mind now if I ask you some questions?"

"Do!" said Mendoza. "That should be tantamount to telling me your conclusions, I should think."

"Why was O'Dell upset Saturday? What was worrying him?"

"You think his being upset had something to do with his death?"

Johnny smiled. "I thought I asked the question."

"What makes you think he was upset? Did I tell you that?"

If you didn t, one of the ladies did. She said she thought O'Dell was worried about a business affair—concerning some bonds."

Mendoza shrugged. "Oh," he said, "Kim wasn't one to worry over business matters. Why *should* he worry? He had two or three millions, and Jervis Ross to look after everything for him."

Johnny leaned forward, gazing at his host's noble profile. "I think Ross was playing around with O'Dell's money. I think he was sending O'Dell false statements concerning his investments. I think O'Dell, just before somebody killed him, found out Ross was lying to him."

"Wonderful!" declared Mendoza. "You have just thrown away the rules. You have revealed to me a simple supposition—one, so far as I can see, without a tittle of evidence to support it. Perhaps you should have specialized in theoretical criminology rather than entering the applied field, dear boy."

A phone tinkled then and in a moment Mendoza's man appeared. "Señor Church, *por favor*," he said. "Long distance on the telephone."

He took the call in the living room and it was Bess. Irene and Ross were listed on a flight out of here to Los Angeles Sunday evening," said Bess. "She had to show her birth certificate to get a tourist card at the Mexican National counter at L.A. airport. So I guess it must have been Mrs. Maybrick in person."

"Thanks, Bess," he said. "See you tomorrow."

They were ready to dine when he went back out onto the terrace. Mendoza, in a friendly, paternal way, took his arm and moved with him to the candlelit table where the servants seated them.

"Hare *en casserole à la Mendoza!* That is the *pièce de résistance* this evening." Mendoza chuckled. "Don't you agree it's a fitting dish? Hare and hounds, you know."

"You must have a good hunter," Johnny remarked.

"The best!" Mendoza told him. "I have never been satisfied with less."

"He must be an excellent marksman."

"The finest in Morelos, Señor Church." Mendoza's eyes glittered at him in the candlelight.

The hare, and all that preceded it, was superb, and once more Johnny was served vintage wines from the cellar of O'Dell. As they finished the hare the phone rang again and Mendoza was summoned.

Angelita came to remove the casserole. "I hope that wasn't *your* rabbit in there," Johnny told her. "The one with the broken ear."

She suppressed a giggle. "No, señor."

"I guess the little boy who gave you the rabbit wouldn't have liked that." He gazed at her. "He's your brother, perhaps?"

"*Sí, señor.*"

"The little one called Tomas, isn't it?"

"*Sí, señor.*"

Mendoza returned. "That was the ladies calling," he said. "They're at your hotel. They are seeking for amusement, or what have you. I told them I was occupied and you weren't here." He giggled. "We have our game to play, don't we? We don't want to be disturbed."

Mendoza clapped his hands and the last dishes were whisked from the table and O'Dell's cigars and Napoleon brandy were placed before Johnny; then Mendoza whispered something to his man, the servants vanished suddenly and they were alone.

As Johnny lifted his brandy he saw her coming slowly toward them, the tray of fruit balanced on her head. There was a pink hibiscus blossom in her hair and she was as she had been when he first saw her, quite nude, the beautiful golden body gleaming in the candlelight.

She knelt before him, offering the tray, her head proudly held, the color high in the masklike face, black lashes lying on her cheeks.

"Now do have fruit!" Mendoza said. "I saw you admiring this little creature yesterday morning, so the fruit is served in this fashion for your pleasure. Was the dinner satisfactory? Are you enjoying the brandy? Dear boy, if there's anything you lack you have simply to ask for it. I want you to be completely happy!"

"No fruit, thank you," Johnny told him. Then he said to the kneeling girl, "Get up, Little Angel."

She did not move, nor give any sign that she had heard him, and when he looked at Mendoza he saw that he was grinning at him. Mendoza snapped his fingers carelessly and, with a perfect, flowing grace, the golden young body came erect and went to kneel beside the old man's chair.

Mendoza selected a grape and popped it in his mouth, then he spat out the seeds. "Now," he declared, "suppose you continue to tell me things. Are we anywhere near to the conclusion you promise for tonight?"

"Yes," said Johnny. "We are. But, first, I have one more question. Do you own a hand gun, Señor Mendoza?"

"Two of them!" Mendoza told him.

"Have you ever fired them?"

"Forgive me," Mendoza said, "if I find that a completely ridiculous question. Of course, I have fired my guns! In my time I have fought four duels with my guns. No gentleman ever dared offend me lightly, I can tell you. When I was a boy, Señor Church, the first thing we young gentlemen were taught was to ride and to shoot. You people, dear boy, see only the surface of this land. You have no conception of the true nature of its people, of the dark and hidden depths within it. I have been through revolutions, in my time—wars, upheavals! And when this present

Populist madness is over I shall regain my lands! Meanwhile, I am always ready, come what may. Would it surprise you to know that beneath the house that was O'Dell's I have a vault containing rifles, hand grenades and machine guns!"

"I guess not," Johnny said.

"I selected this old convent to rebuild with a purpose," Mendoza said. "For in the early days it had to be a fort, as well as a religious sanctuary. I am always prepared, Señor Church. Let them come—revolutionists or alphabet bombs!" He jumped up. "One moment. I will show you what I can do with a firearm!"

Johnny watched him enter his bedroom and snap on the overhead light, saw him skirt the great shrine of a bed on its dais and go to the painting done by Rivera in an earlier, pre-proletarian period. Mendoza swung the painting out from the wall like a door and behind it Johnny saw the face of a fancy old safe. He watched Mendoza's fingers dial the combination, open the safe and remove a mahogany box.

The old gentleman shut the safe, swung back the painting and returned to the table. He placed the box on the table and opened it. Inside, resting in nests of black velvet, were a pair of beautiful old dueling pistols, and there was a silver powder horn, a bullet mould, a ramrod and a silver box for caps. Brass caps were already on the firing nipples of the two pistols, the hammers resting against them; the pistols were loaded.

"My grandfather had these made in Spain," Mendoza said, taking the pistol nearest to Johnny from the box. He spoke sharply to the girl and she rose and placed her tray on the table. She took an apple from the tray and moved down to the end of the terrace, then she turned, placed the apple on her head and froze there, stood poised like some lovely figurine against the wall.

Mendoza took a stance. He raised his pistol, held it pointing upward above his shoulder, cocked it.

"No!" Johnny said.

Mendoza said, "Be quiet, please. I do this all the time. It is an entertainment, understand?"

Johnny took a step toward the girl, but the glance she flashed at him from that masklike face stopped him. She was not afraid of the gun, only afraid that he would make trouble. He sank down in his chair, not wanting to watch her. Mendoza had told him many things, he thought-from him he had learned much. He picked up the other pistol and examined it, cocked it, then let the hammer down on the firing nipple. He had seen the ancient, barbaric symbol of snake and eagle that lurked just out of sight behind the Coca-Cola signs and the façades of the tourist hotels, he thought.

At long last there was the flat *crack* of the pistol and he looked at the girl, saw that the apple had vanished. When Mendoza put the pistol back in the box he picked it up also, hefted the pair of them, then as Mendoza turned to the girl, dismissing her, he replaced both pistols in their velvet nests.

All the bits fit the picture, he thought, and the picture was almost complete. A game had been started in fine style, but a couple of the players had quickly tired. The marksman had returned to his hunting, the little boy had quit riding *libre* bumpers. It reminded him of Jervis Ross's remark the night before about all the unfinished buildings that you saw down there.

CHAPTER SIXTEEN

N OW HE AND MENDOZA were quite alone again, facing each other across the candlelit table.

"I have answered your question," said Mendoza. "Are we ready for your conclusion?"

"Well," said Johnny, "I think both your answer and these guns themselves are irrelevant. My conclusion is that Ross had been playing around with O'Dell's money for a long time. Then O'Dell wanted some particular bonds to put up for security to get a loan for a company down here, some registered, non-negotiable bonds. Ross had gotten rid of those bonds and he couldn't buy more without tilting his hand because all sale and purchase data would be a matter of record on the face of the bonds."

Mendoza looked excited. "How you are *guessing* at things!" he exclaimed. "Heavens—what fantasy!"

"It figures," Johnny said. "Mrs. Maybrick was supposed to have brought those bonds down here. They were supposed to have been stolen. That trick gave Ross stalling time."

"Be careful!" Mendoza warned him. "Remember, you are speaking of the lady I intend to marry, Mr. Church."

"I realize that," Johnny told him. "I also recall you making the statement last night that the lady fascinated you because she was so ruthless." He leaned forward, looking his host in the eye. "I see now what you meant," he told him. "She was playing both ends against the middle, wasn't she?"

"I wish you please would not speak so often in the vernacular!" Mendoza complained. "What do you mean by that?"

"I think she planned to marry Ross, who controls the fortune her boy inherits. But O'Dell was getting suspicious of Ross. Before he could go up there and have a showdown O'Dell *had* to be gotten rid of. So this ruthless lady had an affair with you while she was down here last month. She promised to get Ross to give you back your house, to live there with you as your wife." He paused. "*If* you would get them off the hook by getting rid of O'Dell. Do you understand that vernacular, sir!"

Mendoza laughed. "Oh, please go on!" he begged.

But you didn't trust the lady," Johnny said. "You took the phony reports Ross had been sending O'Dell out of that filecase. You made certain that the bargain you had made with Ross and the lady would be kept!"

Oh, dear me!" Mendoza cried. He leaped to his feet and began pacing rapidly up and down the terrace, his hands plunged into the pockets of his white jacket. Then, finally, he stopped pacing and said, "This is completely a fabric of the imagination you've created, dear boy. A complete fiction!"

"A fiction based firmly on little bits and pieces of factual observation and information," Johnny said. "There was the expression on their faces when the safe was opened, the fact that you saved your big announcement for that moment. There was the empty folder marked 'Ross'." He took the cartridge case from his pocket and tossed it on the table. "And this shell from the gun of your hunter, fired to miss when the game began."

Now he sat gazing steadily at Mendoza, and now he could tell that he, like his hunter and the little brother of the lovely creature who served the fruit, had also tired of the game. It was just another unfinished building. There was also the fact," he said, "that while they tell me you have little money left, you still planned to buy back O Dell's house."

"Who says I have little money left?" Mendoza roared. "Lands I have not, but other wealth—" He stopped in a fury. "Who are some tourists to say what I have?" he went on presently. "Ask those who *know*, dear boy. Ask the Indios, the peasants, retainers, all those families who worked for the Mendozas four centuries of time. They know of the catacombs in this old convent, where once the wealth of the church was stored. They know of *my* wealth—gold, jewels, family treasures, Señor Church. They know of my power!"

"I understand," Johnny told him. He got up. "Well," he said, "the little game is over, as far as I'm concerned. Thanks for an interesting time. Especially the nice little side excursions."

"What are you going to do now?" Mendoza demanded.

"I'm going to go back to San Francisco and tell old lady O'Dell who killed her son."

"Who did?" Mendoza inquired archly.

"I thought I mentioned it," Johnny said. "*You* did."

Mendoza jumped up and down. "No!" he shouted gleefully. "No, no, no! You have lost the game. *I* know who killed him and I shall take you to the man. This very moment I shall!"

"Okay," Johnny agreed slowly, watching him. "Let's go then."

"Right!" Mendoza grabbed up the gun box, dashed into his bedroom with it and came out carrying a large electrical torch. 'We'll need this," he said, and he started off along the terrace.

Their way led them out into the rear court, down the stair and into that vaultlike room where a naked bulb shone above the bloodstained table on which game was prepared; and now the room and the house above them echoed with emptiness. The servants had apparently all gone off—to the carnival, Johnny supposed.

Mendoza crossed to a heavy door, bound with iron. He produced a key, unlocked the door and pulled it open; then, motioning Johnny to precede him, he snapped on the torch and its beam revealed another flight of dark, downward-plunging stone stairs.

Johnny went ahead, the torch lighting the stairs before him; then there was a landing, another iron-bound door. Mendoza unlocked the door, pushed it open and the torch revealed a room that was much like the one above, yet was darker, damper and possessed of a profound and timeless stone despair. There was another door here, which wailed faintly as it was opened and shut with an iron moan behind them; and the torch in this new chamber fell upon a hinged stone slab in the floor. A huge and ancient padlock of chased steel joined an eyelet bolted to the slab and a twin eyelet bolted to the adjacent stone in the floor; and there was a ratchet wheel which wound or unwound a chain fastened to the slab and running through an iron pulley block bolted to the ceiling.

Mendoza set the torch on the floor and unlocked the padlock. "*Now—*" he declared, the echoes of his voice frantically seeking escape. "Wind that wheel!"

Johnny took hold of the handle of the ratchet wheel, put his weight on it and the wheel turned, the chain, with many gruesome and protesting creaks, passed through the pulley block and coiled about the wheel drum. When the slab stood erect Johnny moved over and looked down, sensed depth and horror as the ghastly, rotten-sweet odor came welling up to him.

He looked at Mendoza. "Who was it?" he asked.

"Guess!" Mendoza told him. "You are so clever. You tell me."

Someone you paid," Johnny said.

Mendoza laughed. "No, no, no! Wrong!"

"Anyhow, you fed him well."

Mendoza looked surprised. "How do you know that?"

"If not he wouldn't smell so much quite so soon," Johnny said. "Was he a locksmith maybe?"

"Yes!" Mendoza said. "Right! A *wayward* locksmith." A safe-cracker?"

"Go on! Go on!"

"He killed O'Dell and opened that filecase of O'Dell's for you. Then you brought him down here to get his reward—some of that treasure you don't have."

"Right!" Mendoza cried. "You may go to the head or the class, dear boy. But—the big question is—can you remain there?"

"What do you mean?" Johnny asked him.

"Who was he? Answer that."

Johnny shrugged. "That I wouldn't know."

"So you lose!" Mendoza declared softly. He brought the dueling pistol up from behind his back, and the Spanish steel and the copper cap on the firing nipple winked at Johnny; then there was just the business end of the barrel to look at.

"*Stupid*," whispered Mendoza. "Even the police knew. They told you who it was!"

"*The son of the cook!*"

Mendoza smiled. "Right—but much too late," he said. Then he squeezed the trigger of the pistol and the copper cap made a sharp, little *pop* and sent up a wisp of smoke.

"Well, I guess I *am* stupid," Johnny admitted after a moment. "I took that little cap off and I guess I put it back on the pistol you had just fired at the—"

He didn't get to finish his sentence because the pistol came flying toward his head and he had to duck; and, when Mendoza came lunging after the pistol, he leaped nimbly aside, wanting to get away from that hole in the floor. Then he turned to see the old man, off balance and on tiptoe, teetering at the cavity's brink and for an instant it was anybody's guess whether gravity or Mendoza would win. In the end, gravity and simple justice prevailed. Arms flailing the air, Alonzo Mendoza hastened to join the son of the cook and his scream came welling up to blossom in the cold stone room.

Afterward, there was the slab to lower into place, the padlock to snap; there were the stairs, the doors and then, faintly, he could hear the carnival noise again and his heels echoed on the stone floor of the room where the cubicles and the work table were. Next, he was on the terrace once more, breathing deeply of the warm, fragrant air, and for a moment he gazed up at the moon and stars before he went into Mendoza's room.

He found the bulky file of the Ross-O'Dell correspondence in a large Manila envelope in the safe, and when he had shut the safe and swung the Rivera back in place he turned and saw Angelita standing there, her face no longer masklike, her eyes aflame—and she was still wearing only that pink hibiscus blossom.

For a moment he returned her gaze, then he said softly, "Where are the others?"

"At the carnival, señor," she said.

"You know what has happened?" He could tell from the look in her eyes that she did.

"Sí, señor.

"Has he relatives?"

"Only an old sister, señor."

"Did he ever take journeys?"

"To Acapulco, sometimes—to bathe in the sea," she said.

Say then," he told her, "that he has gone to Acapulco. After two weeks tell his sister that you are concerned because he has not returned."

"Sí, señor," she said.

He moved toward her, stopped before her. "Good-by. Little Angel." He bent to kiss her forehead, but suddenly her arms went around his neck and her damp red lips had found his.

After a moment he dropped the envelope, picked her up and carried her over to that monstrous bed. He pulled the coverlet down and deposited her on the sheet, and he plumped the pillows up behind her head; then he retrieved his envelope and went to the door, and when he turned off the light he could still see her lying there in the moonlight on the great bed, eyes aflame, the blossom glowing palely in her hair.

He walked toward the plaza, and the street was hot and empty, for all the people were down there where the big noise was. When he turned a corner he could see the lights of the Ferris wheel moving against the sky and he thought: Except for this envelope I might just as well have stayed on that wheel and eaten peanuts for the last couple of days.

He passed through the crowd in the plaza, where everything had really begun to jump by that time, and as he entered the hotel the big speaker voice came on again, split the night with another bleating threnody of love.

He had his key in his door before he realized the door was not locked and he was wary when he entered. For a moment he stood listening, then he opened the slats of the blind so that the moon streamed in on the beds, and there was a lady on each bed. Each had draped her gown and her shawl over the back of a chair and they had placed their high-heeled sandals neatly under the chairs. They had ordered drinks, he saw, and then they must have gotten tired sitting around waiting for something to happen, and it had been too hot for clothes.

Since there was no place there for him to lay a weary head, he left them as they were, curled up like two sleepy kittens, the satiny black-haired lady and the velvety blonde, and when he went down and tried the red-haired lady's door it was unlocked and that big voice from the plaza entered the room with him, wailing again of love.

In that room the moon also shone, and he could see her lying like an amber vision, fetchingly arranged, upon the island of the bed.

While he stood gazing at her she opened one eye. "Why don't you turn off the light, honey?" she said.

So he did that. He flipped shut the slats of the blind; and then, in a while, he knew why the late O'Dell had made marital noises at that one, for of the three ladies she certainly had the most.

THE END